Published by Sunasha Creative

The Perfect Daughter Copyright © 2025 by Krutika Surve

ISBN: 979-8-218-71769-8

Cover design by Krutika Surve

Printed in the United States of America

For inquiries, visit https://www.krutikasurve.com/contact

The Perfect Daughter

A Short Story Collection

Written by

Krutika Surve

Dedicated to those chasing the elusive horizon.

Your feet are right where they need to be.

To my parents.

Thank you for making me literate.

Table of Contents

Introduction

Hello. Thank you for taking the time to read this. Allow me to introduce myself.

My name is Krutika Surve.

And I haven't amounted to much in my life.

I am single. I have a job, but an end date seems to inch closer and closer. I have very loving family and friends who I would always go out of my way for.

I live alone in a big city. A city most creatives, like me, tend to flock to for a new beginning.

I believe I am kind, but I wonder for whose sake. Mine or the people around me. (I fear it's the former.)

I am unbelievably lazy. To the point where I skip
numerous meals because I can't be bothered to walk to
the kitchen and microwave something.

I've moved through most of my adult life in solitude, the
silence now more familiar than not. And yet, it seems to
echo.

I take pride in being a multi-hyphenate; although, I am
unremarkable in every aspect. I am a visual artist. A
writer. An actor. There's more but I believe in the rule of
threes. In all endeavors, I've always tried to stay true to
my cultural roots while also trying to forge my own path,
a balance that often feels impossible.

In each of these endeavors, I have barely managed to flutter
above lukewarm success. While others who flocked with
me, have taken flight. Soaring to new heights, while I

cheer from the ground.

And as much as I present myself as this beautiful, kind, and intelligent being to the world. Whether it be regarding a job, a relationship, or even self-care. Someone who is culturally perfect from all angles. There is always something I come back home with. A feeling I didn't have before. A feeling of unsettlement. A feeling of resignation.

Cause as much as I try (or claim to), I end up disappointing myself and the expectations I have created for the person I want to be. From balancing my own identity and the cultural one I belong to.

So, as I navigate through my lackluster journey through adulthood as someone continually missing the mark, something compelled me to build a collection. In my insular world, I wanted to create a series of stories for all the people we are meant to be but always seem to fall short, both in our own lives and in a larger cultural sense. For the people who try their best and yet feel lost, unable to comprehend as to why. For the perfect daughter caught between two worlds, reminding her and them of all the ways they will never be just that. Perfect.

And it is so fucking annoying.

So be it.

San Diego

As she grips the steering wheel, Priya realizes she could simply just leave. The ignition is on. Gear shifted into drive. Her foot resting just enough on the brake. She would just have to move maybe five inches with her toes, and she could just leave. Leave everything behind. Start anew. Maybe she'll move to a sunny place. Somewhere like San Diego. Priya's never been. Maybe she'll start painting. She's always wanted to learn how to paint. But, God, where was the time? She would be able to now. Her packed bags are sitting in the trunk. She could drink like a mad man, sleep with whomever she wants, lay on the warm sand for hours on end. All she would have to do is lift her foot off the brake pedal. Priya can be the sexy and vibrant woman she was destined to be. San Diego would be a sanctuary. San Diego sounds nice.

That's the plan. San Diego.

Priya shifts the gear in park. It sticks a bit, almost as if it's resisting – but that would be absurd. She should probably get it fixed.

She removes her keys from the ignition and walks to the front door of a quaint home. The home is identical to the homes next to it and those homes are identical to the ones next to them. Each clone lined up neatly next to each other for miles.

Actually, the neighborhood is a cul-de-sac. But it *seems* like it could go on for miles. It might as well.

However, unlike the others, this patio is painted in the reflection of the stained glass above the door. A rainbow spills across the two rocking chairs sitting on the chipped wood.

One knock on the door and it swings open. A short, elderly man stands on the other side. His face morphs from shock to pure joy looking at the woman in front of him.

"Hi, Dad."
Her father hugs her tightly.
"Come, come."

She takes off her shoes and her jacket, hanging it in the coat closet. As Priya walks through her father's home, she suddenly feels a bit too big in this small space. Like the walls are inches away from brushing her shoulders. The space is tighter than it was when she was a child, making her movement slower and weighted as she makes her way through the hall.

Her father, however, darts down the hall with impressive speed. The house seemingly warping to accommodate his frame instead of suffocating it. By the time she reaches the kitchen, her father has already put a steel pot of water to boil, pouring spoons of tea powder and sugar.

"Dad, I don't want any tea."

In one ear and out the other. Sighing, she settles herself on the bar stool of the kitchen island. Her father grates ginger into the pot as the water starts to bubble. He finally puts everything down and turns his attention to her. Well, most of it. He still has an eye on the pot of tea.

"To what do I owe this pleasure?"

Priya smiles. Her father has always been loving and welcoming. The most hospitable man. Perhaps, too much so sometimes. He gets tired. It's draining but he'll never show it. Two years after his wife passed and he will continue to treat her guests with so much respect. He'll laugh at their jokes, listen to their stories, make them tea. Every one of them would look at her father and simply see a spark of positivity. But Priya knows better. He's lost color from the lack of sun. His socks have holes in them from overuse. The air within the house is stale – thick with dust built up over time.

"I just wanted to see you." He places his hand over his heart.

"Thank you, beta. I've missed you."

"I've missed you, too. I just wanted to check in. I haven't come down in a while."

"And whose fault is that?"

"Mine, I know."

"Shameless." He clicks his tongue, and Priya laughs softly.

"But you're busy, I understand. I hope Rohit is helping with the kids."

She draws a sharp breath. Almost as if she just remembered her husband and two children.

"Yeah, he helps. But two people can only do so much."

"*Arey*, bring them here. I'll happily look at them. You guys go on a date or something."

"Yeah, that would be nice."

"Don't even ask. Just drop them off. Don't even have to come inside. I have CCTV now, I'll keep an eye out."

The pot of tea starts to erupt. The bubbles are just about to pour over the edges as her father pours milk, bringing the boil down. He turns off the gas and sieves the tea into two mugs. He hands his daughter the cup of tea. She places her entire palm on the side of the mug. The warmth settles into her skin, bringing her hand to life. Priya thinks of the San Diego sand how it would warm the same hand. She won't take a sip yet. Right now, she'll just indulge in the warmth seeping into each of pore of her hand and into the veins – though it doesn't go far. Suddenly, she's aware of the chill that cascades over the rest of her body.

"Dad."

"Did you hear Kavya is getting married?" Her cousin. She's 23. She's her dad's brother's daughter.

The last Priya remembers of her was when she was maybe 10 or 11, asking her to take her to the store to buy a book.

"What?"

"Yes, everything is fixed. I'm hoping to book tickets to India. Just need to confirm a date."

"Isn't she young?"

"She's got her MBA. A good job. She's old enough."

A beat goes by.

"She's a bit young."
"You were 24. How's that any different?"

She takes a sip of the tea, slightly burning her lip.
"How long have they been engaged for?"
Her father shrugs, "two, three months?"
"But maybe they should prolong the engagement? Take a breather."
"Why?"

Priya didn't have an answer to her father. All she knows is…if she had the chance she would've waited.

Priya loves her husband. Truly. Rohit was the smartest kid in their Business Analytics 101 class first semester of their freshman year. Priya may not have been the brightest, but she was charming as hell. And Rohit ate it up like cake. They would frequently have study sessions. Throughout their sessions, they would sit in the common room and Rohit would recap the lecture. For some reason, the lessons seemed so much more digestible when they came from him instead of their pretentious professor — who was presumably there just to sell his book. Priya started to understand their assignments and suddenly she wanted more from the person sitting across from her. After each study session, she would learn a new piece of him:

He has an older sister.
He was born in Michigan.
He doesn't like mushrooms.

And she would hold onto it until the next week and the

cycle would continue. Too bad all she would ever see of his face was the bridge of his nose and his bushy eyebrows permanently furrowed. His head was always looking down. Priya often wondered how he never had any neck or back problem.

The weekly study sessions weren't enough. She would frequently wait by the door after their lecture, hoping to bump into him. One day, she eventually did. And seemingly for the first time in his life, Rohit looked up and their eyes met. Suddenly everything about him became…human. He felt real. Tangible. Presence weighed down by gravity. And he must've noticed too. Cause after that, they didn't leave each other's side. What had started as a strategy to ace her class ended with Priya falling for the nerd. Rohit was shy and mostly kept to himself. Priya's energy was nothing short of electric. While Rohit helped her with school, Priya pulled him out of the bubble he lived in. He grounded her, and she lifted him up.

They had their differences, sure. Priya worried she wasn't smart enough for him. Rohit worried he wasn't fun enough for her. And yet, it worked. For every silence he produced, she'd fill it with laughter. And for every thought spilling out of her, he's listened and absorbed.

It was the story they would tell every new person they met.

They finished their bachelor's. They attended different graduate programs in different states, and while the long distance was hard, they made it work with phone calls and frequent flier miles. Priya knew the second they received that stupid piece of paper at graduation, she would get to be with him. And once again, she would not leave his side. Priya and Rohit told their respective parents about their love for one another. That they've started applying to jobs in the same cities.

A bit reckless on their part, Priya would think, because almost immediately their parents started discussing an impending marriage. Though abrupt, Priya and Rohit did love one another and accepted their fate. They got married in a grand affair six months later. And in the eleven years they've been married, they popped out two kids. Boys – nine and five years old.

"Maybe I'll go for a month. Haven't been there since…"

Her father doesn't finish the sentence. Priya nods understandably.

"Yeah, you should go. I'm sure everyone misses you."

"We haven't had a wedding in a while. I better practice some freestyle dance steps."

"How long has Kavya dated her fiancé?"

"I believe they were schoolmates and were good friends. But it was arranged."

"Why?"

"What do you mean "why?""

"Like why now then? What's the rush?"

"No rush but she is a beautiful, young woman. Plus, this boy seems nice. He's an NRI. They are planning to move to Chicago after the wedding."

"Oh."

"Isn't it exciting?"

"Sure, but isn't it …wouldn't she be upending her world? She's been in India her entire life." "But the States will provide her a better life."

"Bombay is a pretty advanced city, Dad. She's really not missing much." "Of course, but he lives in Chicago. He has a job there."

A beat passes.

"Do you not want her to get married?"
"What? Of course, I do. I just wonder if it's too early."

"Did you feel like it was too early for you?"

Priya sits up.
"Sometimes."

"You were together for six years."

She forgot how long they dated for. Not because of its irrelevance but because her college years flew by so quickly. While Rohit consistently kept his head down, her head was up toward the skies — lost in thought. It wasn't until her thirties, Priya realized she never paid attention to her surroundings. If you asked her of any memories from her college years, she could tell you three stories: how her and Rohit met, the time she pulled an all-nighter at a party and found herself waking up in a grocery store cart at nine in the morning and the time Rohit surprised her during grad school for their anniversary. Everything else is a muddled mess. Studying, crying, sex, more studying, more crying, still the same amount of sex and the god-awful taste of Burnett's. Her faulty memory is also a constant issue with Rohit, who has the closest thing to an eidetic one.

"I know but I…" Priya couldn't find the words.
"Is everything okay with him?"
"What?! Yes! Of course, he's…he's a good father and –"
"Is he a good husband?"
"Yes, dad."

Priya almost scoffs at the absurdity of the question. Of course, he's a good husband. He loves his wife and his kids.

He helps around the house. He provides. He's caring and kind. Their sex life is consistent enough. He maintains all the good masculine qualities and very few of the bad ones. Sometimes, she still gets butterflies when he does something endearing. Sometimes.

Then again, Priya doesn't know why she would've wanted to wait.

"I know I would've married him eventually. Maybe…maybe just not straight after grad school."

Her father stares at her baffled. She might've been speaking another language.

"I don't know if that makes sense." Priya tries to look her father in the eye.

"It doesn't."

"There are just responsibilities with being a wife and a mother."

"As there are with anything and everything you do."

"And I wonder if those responsibilities could've been pushed out?"

"Why?"

It's at the tip of her tongue but she cannot find the words. Does she even know why?

"Have you ever been to San Diego?"

"What? No, I don't think so."

"I haven't. But it looks so nice."

"You and Rohit planning on taking the kids?"

"No…just me."

Priya's father looks at her. Priya sees him process her statement. The silence between lingers.

"When are you going?"

"I don't know yet."

Silence.

"Will you be back to come with me to Kavya's wedding?"

More silence.

And more.

"Your tea is cold."

Priya looks down at her mug. She's taken maybe one sip. "Shall I warm it for you?"

Priya looks back up at her father.

"No, it's fine. I told you I didn't want tea, Dad." She walks to the sink and starts to pour the tea down the drain.

"It'll go to waste."

"One cup won't hurt."

Her father stares at her. He was never an angry man. Nor a verbal one. Her mother was the one to discipline. "Ok," is all he says.

Priya looks at her father. "I should get going."
"You drove an hour only to leave after 30 minutes?"

Priya sighs. A sharp pain erupts in her head.

"I have a headache, and the kids will be home soon."
"Okay."
"Okay, then."
"When are you going to San Diego?"
"Tonight."
"Oh."
"Yeah, a bit last minute on my part."
"Rohit will be home with the kids?"
"Yes. But we will need your help if that's okay."

"Of course."

"Thank you."

"When are you coming back?"

Priya stares at her father. She can feel the tension in her chest. She controls every muscle in her face to stay composed, pulling at each tendon to ensure her face doesn't crumple as she speaks.

"I don't think I am."

"I don't understand."

Those tendons, pulling taught, one snaps.

"I can't go back, Dad." She breathes out.

He stares at her for a moment then takes his finished mug to the sink and starts to wash it. He takes his time. Lathers the mug with soap, scrubbing every inch. He rinses it out and puts it on the drying rack.

He takes Priya's empty mug left in the sink. And repeat. All Priya can do is wait and watch her father. She wouldn't dare utter another word until he does.

"Has he hurt you?"

"No, god, of course not."

"You'll tell me if he has?"

"Yes, but he hasn't."

"Then what's wrong?"

"I just can't go back, Dad!"

"Does Rohit know?"

Priya doesn't respond.

"Does Rohit know, Priya?"

Her voice shakes. "No."

He sighs. Priya would hope he would understand. But he won't. He'll keep quiet and be the ideal host. He'll bite his tongue, though family is everything. People will gossip. Her family would be hurt. Rohit would be hurt. The kids will be hurt. And he won't understand. None of them will.

"Dad."

"What?"

"Can you please say something?"

"What is there to say?"

"I don't know."

"Do you want me to talk you out of it?"

Priya hesitates a moment before shaking her head.

"Then there's nothing to say."

"I need you to understand."

"I won't."

She knows.

"I have been in this house for 40 years. It is the only home I have ever owned. And it's the only home I will ever own. This was the first house I came to in the U.S. The first house I brought my wife to. Your mother. The house where we raised our children. The house where we held countless pujas and parties. The house where she died. And now it's just me and the house."

Priya loves this house. As tight and small as it is now, that much will always be clear.

"It's too big for me now. It's difficult to maintain. And yet, I cannot bare leaving it."

Priya tries to find reason even though something is telling her not to.

"It's just a house, Dad."

"It's a part of my life. It's old. The pipes burst every winter. But I'll never leave it."

"I love this house too," she whispers.

"They are a part of your life. They are certainly worth more than any house, Priya."

"They are."

"Then what are you doing?"

Her breath catches. "I'm so tired."

"So am I."

"No, I am tired. Me! I know everyone else is too, whatever the reason may be. But I can only feel what I am feeling, and I'm exhausted. I don't even recognize myself anymore."

"Of course, you don't."

"No! Dad! I can't be tired!"

Priya presses her fingers to her temple. Something threatening to pour out if she doesn't keep her head physically together.

"I *never* got a break. It was straight from school to marriage to kids."

Baffled would be an understatement for her father. He did the same after all. "And?"

"And…"

"How's that different from anyone else?"

"People got a chance to be with themselves. I've…never been alone in my life, Dad."

"You think that's a good enough reason to leave your husband and your kids?"

She is taken back by it. By the bluntness of his statement. After all, that is the conversation that they are having. And yet, she's shocked. She's surprised.

"I've never lived on my own."

"Ok…"

"No, I've never – not once – done my own taxes. You would do them and then Rohit does them. I have never once done them on my own."

"Then learn how to do them. Do them next year."

"That's not the point, Dad. I've never *had* to do them. I've never had to fix the pipe under the sink. Or jumpstart my car. Or clean the gutters. You did. Then Rohit did. I've never once been independent in my life. I don't even know if I can be. Be my own person. And now I'll never know."

Priya takes a deep breath but doesn't release it. She can barely see him through her clouded eyes.

"You're a wife and a mother."

"So, that's all I am?"

"You're my daughter."

"No! Dad, I am a person. A whole being. But everything I've been resorted to is who I am to other people."

Her father exhales. "I understand."

"You do?"

"Everybody deals with this at your age – "

"Dad!"

"It's completely natural."

"No, Dad! You don't get it. Ever since Rohit and I got engaged…I've been feeling like something was off. Like I was in a room with no windows. The room would have everything, a bed, a closet, a freaking humidifier but it wouldn't have any windows. It would have everything else but that. And I didn't say anything. Only to find out a room without windows is absolutely suffocating. I love Rohit. I love my kids. But I...I've never been alone. Not once in my entire life."

"Are you not ashamed?!"

Priya's father was not one to raise his voice. Compared to the fire of her mother, he was the calm, the steady voice of reason.

Priya could still remember the only time he ever yelled at her. She was sixteen and had a crush on a boy—the kind of boy who set off every parental alarm. He was reckless, careless, and failing most of his classes. He did whatever he wanted, without a thought for the consequences. He was attractive and he knew it. But more than that, he was magnetic. He knew how to talk, how to look at you just long enough to make you feel seen. And somehow, he noticed Priya. She didn't understand why, but it filled her with a dangerous kind of pride.

They started talking often, slipping notes to each other during class. Her parents didn't say much, though they kept their boundaries. They reminded themselves she was young, and some things she'd have to figure out for herself.

Then came the party—her first. He invited her, and she didn't ask for permission. She already knew what the answer would be. She snuck out instead, wearing a skintight black dress that ended just below her rear. When she looked in the mirror, it was like seeing her body—really seeing it—for the first time. She stood taller, her shoulders back. A new palette of browns, purples, and golden glitter lit up her eyes. And for the first time, Priya felt beautiful. For the first time, she understood why someone like him might want someone like her. And that was a powerful feeling—terrifying, thrilling, unforgettable.

The party was nothing like Priya had seen in movies. It was relatively tame. People were chatting amongst themselves, drinking God knows what. But with the music, the dancing, the laughter, it was perfect. Priya cannot count how many friends she made that night. She didn't drink much so she remembers everything. That girl from her chemistry class who had become one of her best friends. The way that boy's hand consistently rested on her lower back. The bloody foyer of the house. She remembers him fidgeting in the car on the way back to her house. There's nothing more enthralling than watching someone who exudes confidence unravel in the slight pull of your presence. The way he hesitated, looking into her eyes for confirmation before leaning across the console to kiss her. Something inside of her short-circuited and caught on fire. She never felt more alive.

In a daze, she stumbled through the hall of her house, a small smile stamped on her face. Her father sat at the kitchen island, dressed in an elegant kurta. Her mom in a beautiful saree sat the dining table eating a small piece of cake. In all the excitement, Priya had missed her mother's birthday dinner. And her father was enraged. Her mother's 40th birthday dinner had been planned for weeks and all their family friends convened at a family friend's house. Dressed in expensive sarees and kurtas, each with a dish in hand. If you ask her now, Priya still feels a bit guilty, but she moved on. But at the time, you would think she committed a murder. Her father's voice had never been louder. Just the sheer volume sent chills down her spine. He was worried, scared that they didn't know where their daughter was. Then furious when they saw that she didn't care. She was used to her mother's raised tone. She would yell at anything. She was one to emote first then process later. Her father carefully gathered each part of a situation and handled things according. But now her father… she was afraid. Not of her father but her father's disappointment. How could she have forgotten? How could she disrespect her family like this? How could she abandon her family?

Her father's voice was not as loud now as it was then. But it rumbled as if he was attempting to hold everything in.

"I'm suffocating."

Her father walks around the kitchen. An exasperated hand pulls at his loose skin as he drags it down his face.

"You cannot leave."
"What?"

"You feel suffocated? Do something about it but do not leave your family. If you want a divorce…"

"I don't."

"Have some respect, Priya. At least have the respect to divorce your husband. You can figure out custody and where to live– "

"No! Dad, I don't want any of it!"

Her fingers touch her lips, trying to find those horrible words that spilled out of them.

"You have a responsibility, Priya."

"I've had nothing but responsibilities."

"You will not escape them. If it's not this, then it'll be something else." He takes a deep breath. "Don't do this to them."

"They'll be fine without me."

"No, they won't."

"You are their mother! You are his wife. A pillar. You're needed. I need you. You are *loved*, Priya." He was now at birthday dinner volume, and suddenly, Priya was sixteen once again.

Priya didn't even realize she was sobbing until she felt her breath catch, once, twice, three times.

"You have a family, Priya. People have lost their loved ones, and you have them. How can you just leave?"

"It's not the same."

"But it is! It is!"

Priya has never seen her father cry before. Even when her mother passed, he never cried in front of her and her sister. Not once. They would sob, act out, dissociate. And he just stood by them., but he never did anything in front of them. He would go to bed at night and let it all out. Blinded by her own grief, Priya would have never known if Rohit hadn't saw him one night.

Tears fill her father's eyes. His speech, a bubbling mess.

"You are intelligent. You…you are not happy. But do something about it."

"I am."

"NOT THIS! Anything but this, Priya. Your happiness will not be worthwhile if it's going to be at the cost of them."

Priya shakes her head.

"You think this will help? You will hate yourself, Priya. You cannot leave the life you have just to lead something else. They will not forget, and you will not forget. You will miss your husband. You will miss your children. You love them? Then prove it. Stay. Find a solution where you're all happy. But if you love yourself more than them then I cannot say anything."

Priya can only stare at her father. Every inch of her wants to resist. Wants to deny and protest, but she cannot find the words—words of reason. Are there any?

"It's astounding how they cannot be enough for you."

Her father wipes the tears from his face. He straightens and wipes his hands on his dated tracksuit. "Do what you want, Priya. I believe I have raised you right. That you will make the right decision."

Her father walks down the hall to the front door. Priya silently follows. She dares to meet his gaze as she steps out.

"I love you, Dad."

He sighs. "I love you, beta."

Priya sits back into her car. The breath she had been holding releases itself, coming out in spurts as she breaks down in sobs. She doesn't recognize her voice. That wailing noise coming out of her mouth. She thinks of her mother. The pain she saw in her eyes that day she wasn't there. She couldn't bear to see that in Rohit's. In her children's. She looks at her the passenger seat of the car. It was her seat. Rohit sits at the wheel. The kids in the back. She remembers the trip to the Grand Canyon. The kids were babies. They fell asleep and Rohit and her would listen to 90s Bollywood on a low hum. She remembers looking at her kids sleeping soundly in the back—their cheeks pressed against the car seats. The four of them were sitting silently. At peace.

Priya turns on the ignition and shifts the car into drive. The gear sticks again. She really needs to get that fixed.

She'll get it fixed in San Diego.

Relevant Experience*

*(or lack thereof)

Her mom would have a proper heart attack if she ever saw this outfit. She would never, though. That, Rajvi can absolutely guarantee. Those photos she and her friends took during the pre-game would never see the light of day—not with this top, not with all the skin, and definitely not with the bottles of liquor sitting in the background.

She never had nights like this. Not in high school. Not in college. Not in grad school. Not when her education consumed all her time and energy. Education and career above all. That was always the priority. But now with a master's degree and a well-paying job, she's done it. All her work has been worthwhile. She got the grades, and she was rewarded handsomely. The rigorous all-nighters, the stress, the crying. It was worth it. It gave her everything she could ever hope for. And now, at 25, she's the definition of success. Her parents couldn't be any happier. Rajvi has become the ultimate role model.

Rajvi pulls her skirt down, trying to find what little coverage she can get. It's embarrassing. How out of touch she feels in this new skin. The top and skirt are her roommate's, Ira. They met on Facebook. Rajvi had never seen or met someone as beautiful as her. Her features are soft and light; the way she carries herself was anything but. She's dynamic and ultimately the most captivating person in every room, and Rajvi can't help but envy her. How boys craned their necks for her; how the girls admired her; and it was Rajvi attached to her hip. Wearing her clothes, with her makeup painted on her face. Ira would whisper something in her ear and Rajvi would stand taller. Something about the privilege of being Ira's friend felt like proximity to a celebrity.

A guy walked up to them, standing tall and confident. Offered to buy Ira a drink.

"Sorry, I'm just here for a girl's night. Thanks!"

It was all she said to get that boy to turn around and walk the other way. Short and sweet. Rajvi assumed she was offered a drink many times. Ira wouldn't mind, though. She politely declines then goes on regarding some story about "some bitch named Emily".

Ira seemed to know everything.

"Make eye contact with him, small smile, and then look away. You want to be interested but not enough. And if they're dumb and can't tell you're interested, look at them again," she tells Rajvi.

"What if they aren't into me?" Rajvi asks.

"Oh, don't give them credit, men would fuck a corpse if they could."

A laugh bursts out of Rajvi.

"Not that you're like a corpse, I'm just saying they'd be so lucky to have you even look at them."

With that given confidence, Rajvi looks around the crowded bar. The faces blurred. They all look the same. 20-something, white, and wearing slim-fit pants. They sip their drinks. Laugh. Bopping their heads to the vague thumping spitting out of the speakers. She finds herself doing a double-take on a man. He's young but seems pensive. The way he listens to his much louder friends laugh and chatter amongst themselves, digesting whatever nonsense they were no doubt spouting. He's casually dressed but dressed well. His hair, however – the curls had a mind of their own. Rajvi didn't even realize she was staring until Ira bumped her shoulder playfully, urging her to make a move. She wouldn't, though. She doesn't even know how. Rajvi shrugged her off and continued to sip lightly from her vodka cranberry.

She's been on her own for maybe a month and this is the first time she's lived on her own. Throughout her school and college days, she lived at home with her parents and two younger sisters. As studies were her focus, boys and a social life fell far away. They were trivial— at least that's what she would say to others. While everyone was having their firsts, she sat quietly in her room – studying, or, perhaps, watching a reality television show if she was feeling crazy. Rajvi is not proud of being a 25-year-old virgin. Ira would tell her it's nothing to be ashamed of. That everyone has their own timelines.

"You're not missing much." She would joke.

But as someone always at the top of her class, Rajvi never felt so behind. Ira has slept with her fair share of guys. She knows what to do and when to do it. She knows how to make herself feel good. She knows how to make them squirm. Whoever that would be. Ira told her about the night she lost her virginity: She was 17. One of her friends had thrown a kickback after a graduation party. This friend was older than Ira. He was "handsome and dumb". The tether was inexplicable. She needed to figure him out. What was so special about him? If you ask Ira now, she'll simply answer "horniness". But at the time, she couldn't comprehend that connection. After some heavy drinking, everyone had laid next to each other to go to sleep. Ira remembers reaching over and tapping that boy. By the time he turned toward her, she had pretended she was asleep. He nudged her and she "woke up". Her first time was painful. Not because of him. But because of her. Because her body was not as ready as her brain was.

Rajvi felt like a child in her midst. It didn't matter how educated she was. Her ranking. Her position. Her salary. She's out of her depth. In this deep cut top and short skirt, sipping sugar and acetone. This isn't her. But she wants it to be. The sexual prowess and confidence of her roommate. The pure heat that lingers in her wake.

She looks back at the young man. His laughter carried across the room. Rajvi wondered if she would laugh at the same joke.

Would he be caring and loving? Or would his attention be something she'd have to fight for?

He's American. Would he crumble under the weight of her culture? Would he embrace the color and vibrance of it? How will he look in a sherwani?

Why is she thinking about him in a sherwani?

He catches her gaze. Rajvi immediately looks away, shaking out the picture of him in a sherwani with those curls shoved poorly inside a pheta. Back at Ira, whose gaze is elsewhere. She turns back to him only to see him walking over.

To her?
No.
Oh shit, yeah, to her.

Before Rajvi can contemplate her next steps, he is standing in front of her. Ira finds herself taking several steps away to give her friend some space. He's not very tall but she still has to look up to meet his eyes. They're blue. She doesn't understand why that excites her.

"I ran out of product." He speaks over the music.

"What?"

"You keep looking at my hair. I ran out of product."

Her neck is cramping with how high her shoulders shot up. He just came up to her. He saw her staring and then just came up.

"Oh."

"I'm John."

Americans are effortlessly confident. Obliviously so. They don't think. They just do. Rajvi recalls how the boys in high school would just…do. How they spoke up in class. They would never raise their hands or wait patiently for the teacher to call their name. They just spoke. Something stupid. And the class would laugh. The teacher would brush it off. And they would move on. Even in her office, her colleagues would just do. They say whatever. They do whatever. And then…they go home. And come back the next day and do the same.

Granted, Rajvi is American too, but not in the same way. Not in the way that feels like the identity is wholly hers, finding it laced with expectation and compromise. Regardless of her being born and raised in the country, the sense of belonging feels conditional.

It baffles Rajvi. How they unapologetically take up space with no regard for the people around them. Unapologetic and unburdened. The air around them bending to their form. The lack of discipline. And more importantly, the lack of consequence.

How if she spoke like that, even in the comfort of her own home, she would be disciplined. Her parents were caring. And loving. So ever loving, but they were particular. They had a regimen for their children. They had standards for their children. Dinner at 7, if you were late, you'd eat at 5 the next morning. They would quiz her at random on SAT words at the age of twelve. Tennis lessons at 9 every Sunday morning for activity.

It was just as much work on them as it was for Rajvi. Rajvi was no more than an extension of them—their dreams. Americans would probably deem them strict. Perhaps, a good thing. Their hard work is evident in her.

"What's your name?"

Her breath catches, and her chest constricts for a millisecond. Not in excitement but in unease. It always does when someone asks for her name. Especially someone non-Indian. And in a loud environment like this? It feels futile to even try.

"Rajvi."

"Sorry?" He leans closer. Does he not understand personal space?

She swallows. A little louder. Enunciating each syllable dramatically.

"Raj-vee."
"Rajvi?"

Her shoulders are somehow lower than they were a second ago. She nods.

"That's pretty." Every foreign name is in America.
"Thank you."
"It's nice to meet you." He smiles and holds out his hand.

"You, too." She shakes it.

"Can I buy you a drink?"

Rajvi looks to her friend, now a good ten paces away from her. She rewards her with a proud smile. Rajvi turns back to John and to her now empty drink.

"Sure."

His smile, even wider. "What do you like?"

She doesn't know. She would pick the easiest thing. A shot of vodka and cranberry juice. That's what Ira gave her at the beginning of the night. Rajvi knows she doesn't like beer. Nor wine. Nor any dark liquor. But a vodka cranberry feels juvenile.

"A martini."

He nods and orders. The bartender hands her the drink. It tastes like knives. Sharp slashes as the warmth cascades down her throat. She hides her disgust as well as she can.

"Are you having a good night?"

Rajvi is not antisocial. In fact, she's not even shy. She's lively. Charismatic. Her friends back home always thought of her as the rowdy one. But as an adult, next to people like Ira and John, she's quiet and demure. She hates it. How weak it makes her feel. She's pretty and smart. She can make people laugh. But not here. Not with him.

"Yeah, I'm kind of tired though."
"Tired?! It's only 11."
"I'm a morning person."
"Oh jeez, I'm jealous. It takes me a solid 40 minutes to get out of bed. I have to set my alarm an hour earlier."

How would that work? If they lived together? Is he lazy? Would he not work for his family? If John's eyes would leave her for at least just one second, she would pinch herself.

Why is she thinking about him like this?

She wishes she could say it's just some intrinsic connection she has with him. Like something just snapped. Romance right out of a book. But it's not. He's just someone of the opposite sex. The type she's never had experience with. All she would have to do is make eye contact with someone and an entire life would flash behind her eyes. It happens at work, at the grocery store, on a plane as they are standing in the aisle to get to their seat. She wonders if she creates alternate realities with each fantasy. The type of fantasy she consumes through pages or a screen. Who would

John be? Who would Rajvi be with John? What would their kids look like?

She tries to focus on their conversation. He's so animated when he talks. Like he actually wants to talk to her. He asks about her family, her work. His own questions ricochet back to him. He has one brother. His parents are divorced. He's in law school.

She likes him. He's kind and funny. Her walls inch their way down as their conversation continues. Like they are friends.

He must've noticed the shift in comfort in the woman across from him. He inches closer, ever so slowly. Letting the tip of his index touch her arm.

There was a time when Rajvi was comfortable with physical touch. Somewhere along the line, they became foreign to her. She remembers the time a boy—an old family friend—sat next to her at dinner. He pushed his knee against hers under the table. Rajvi was certain he wanted her. He never came forward about his supposed undying love for her. Ass.

And perhaps, that was the issue. Rajvi, to this day, is sure that the touch was deliberate. It couldn't have been accidental or fleeting. And yet, it meant nothing. So now, even the smallest gesture of touch feels like something to brace for. Something to question or second-guess. She doesn't even hug or cuddle. Doesn't matter if they are her friends or her family. The extent of her touch can go as far as a handshake, but sometimes even that felt too intimate. Rajvi wonders if something is wrong with her. If she has some sort of brain injury. She tries to convince herself that she doesn't, that she's not used to it. But nonetheless, her focus goes to that singular touch of the index.

Rajvi just wants to feel beautiful. Like Ira. Like her American friends. She wants to be touched. She wants to feel pleasure. Why wouldn't she? It's a normal biological reaction, is it not? And though she's confident in her own right, she does seek some part of it from male validation. John thinks of her as someone worth pursuing. It shouldn't inflate her sense of presence. But it does.

John and Rajvi continue to converse. Rajvi forces herself to lean into his touch. She won't lie, it doesn't feel right. It feels unequivocally invasive. But this is what flirting is, right? How would she ever move on from being a 25-year-old virgin if she didn't push herself? How can she catch up with her peers and with people like Ira?

Rajvi remembers the days of studying. Her tactic was impenetrable. And it worked. Everyone knows it worked.

She would read each chapter and after each chapter, she would write a synopsis in a notebook of what she had read. If she couldn't understand it enough to write on it, she would read it again. And again. And again. Until she understood, until it was so ingrained in her brain, she wouldn't be able to think of anything else until she finished writing her chapter synopsis. And then repeat for the next one.

It was tedious, she won't lie. There were times when she wondered if there was a better way to understand some topics. But that's the way she was taught by her parents. As was everything. Naturally, her parents didn't teach her anything about sex. That was just something she learned in school and kept to herself. She recalled how she never even saw her parents hold hands and how baffling it was that they even procreated.

She treated Ira like a chapter as respectfully as she could. Something she could read repeatedly until she can reflect her habits and body language on her own. That was all she could do. Whenever she was overwhelmed in class, she returned to her tried and true to understand what was lost upon her until she caught up.

Ira would touch their arm.

Rajvi touches John's arm.

Ira would laugh at their joke (even if they weren't funny).

John says something about a fiasco at his internship. Rajvi laughs.

Ira would inch slower, provoking them to touch her.

Rajvi moves a half step closer to John. He doesn't seem to notice until he takes that index finger and wraps his whole hand around the back of her arm.

"How's your drink?"

"It's really bad!" Rajvi laughed. He laughs as well.

This flirting nonsense is going great.

He touches her waist—she could barely tell it's there. He leans even closer. She hadn't even known there was even more space between them that hadn't possibly been taken up already.

Rajvi looks around. She doesn't know how to move forward. She looks to her friend who was talking to another man but was undoubtedly keeping an eye on her new roommate. She gives her a wary and cautious smile.

Are you okay?

Rajvi sighs and smiles back. *I'm good. Are you?*

Ira returns a reassuring smile back to her friend. *Yes, I am.*

She turns back to John.

He was going to kiss her. She doesn't move, allowing him all the power in this decision. As his eyes drift to a close, hers dart back and forth from around the bar. Either more people came in the last 40 minutes, or it was smaller than she thought.

Before she could register, his lips met hers. He keeps working at it. She doesn't know what to do but let instinct take over. She gets even closer to him. A spark of pride shoots through her. She knows Ira would be practically squealing. This man wants her. He wants her. Out of all the girls in the bar, he chose her. Made her comfortable. Took his time. She didn't know his last name. His favorite color. His political leanings. But it didn't matter. She feels wanted…and it begs the question, "Why?"

She leans back. Away from the hand around her arm. Away from the hand that rested on her waist. The alarm was evident in his eyes at the abrupt halt.

"I-I'm so sorry."
Rajvi didn't say anything.
"I misread…I'm so sorry."

She suddenly is rushed with a wave of guilt. She's been giving him the signs all night. The way Ira instructed her to do it. She wanted to do it. She wanted to be kissed. To be devoured. And suddenly, when the opportunity presented to her, she felt herself crawl back into her skin. The skin of the scholar. The one who succeeds. The perfect daughter.

"No, no I – I just didn't know what was happening." She laughs as an attempt to put him at ease.
"I'm sorry. I'm kind of drunk."

"It's okay. No, I'm sorry. It's just… there are a lot of people around. I don't want to creep them out." They both laugh.

"Did I fuck this up?"

"No, no."

He would understand, won't he? He seems reasonable. This would be something to laugh at once they are old and grey. If it ever came to that point.

"I'm sorry. I've just…"

She struggles to find the words. She was never truly very articulate. She was good at memorization and seeing things in front of her. But with concepts such as lust, she couldn't comprehend.

"It was nice meeting you, John."

"Wait, are you okay?"

"Yes, sorry. I think…I kind of ditched my friend. And I think we are about to head out. It's not you, I promise."

She laughs off her discomfort, but she can see it in his eyes. The rejection. If only he knew that he was the first to pull her out of hiding. And that she only stretched too far.

"Oh, okay…"

She felt guilty. Ira made rejection look effortless. But evidently, Rajvi cannot. Nor does she want to. Something tells her that John would respect the pacing she would allow herself. Perhaps, she's delusional. Or perhaps, he is that man in the sherwani.

"How about I get your number?"

John processes what she said for a moment before giving his phone to her.. They type their respective information into the devices and hand them back to one another. John gives her a big smile. He has a nice smile. Rajvi reaches for a hug. A hug she can do. He embraces her tightly – a message she would think. To use the number typed into her phone.

She reaches for her bag and looks back at Ira. Ira makes eye contact with her and immediately stands up, expertly brushing off the man that has been occupying half of her attention. The two make their way towards the door.

Done with the night. First of many, she would presume. More chances for her to slowly crawl out of the person she has built herself up to be her entire life into the woman she wants to be.

Rajvi turns back to look at John. He went back to his friends, but managed to keep an eye on the door, making eye contact once again with his new acquaintance. She gives a small smile goodbye.

Leaving

Everyone else goes to bed early, but my grandmother and I stay up. She applies mehndi to my hand, the scent filling the room. We talk nonsense until we grow tired, then fall asleep next to each other on her bed, waiting for a new day.

When I wake up, a packed bag sits at the foot of the bed. It doesn't matter whose it is — someone is leaving for a long time. I'll probably see them again, but in that moment, I forget.

My grandmother, having gotten up at the crack of dawn, I presume, walks into my room. She asks what I want for breakfast and tells me I should probably take a bath before we start the washing machine. Begrudgingly, I get up and fold the comforter I slept with. Someone is leaving for a long time.

I walk into the other rooms, searching for anyone. In the kitchen, my mother tapes the lid onto a jar filled with some random spice while my aunt and cousin sister help her. Several filled jars crowd the floor, each taped up and wrapped for the long journey—because someone is leaving for a long time.

I glance into the living room, where my father, grandfather, brother, and cousin brother sit watching the news. How typical of men.

I turn back to the packed bags, sitting idly at the foot of the bed, waiting to be shoved into the trunk of a car. The driver will play Tetris with them. Someone is leaving. For a long time.

How can I eat and shower when someone's leaving for a long time? We'll be 8,000 miles apart. When it's day, it's night; and when it's night, it's day. And it breaks my heart every time.

And now that I'm older, it's no longer that someone is leaving for a long time. It's that someone is leaving and will never come back. And I would never know the last time is the last time. Until I get a call in my apartment, alone in a big city.

They were supposed to leave for a long time. And yet, they never came back. No more late nights filled with the scent of mehndi and nonsense. Only six weeks out of the year, if that. And then someone would be coming back—for a short time, but a time, nonetheless.

I imagine a life where I stay. Where would I go to school? What would I do on the weekend? Who would I socialize with? Would I be treated differently? Would I be a different person?

But I would be home with the ones I love.

And every day, I wake up—it's just a new day. And that,
for once, someone would stay.

The Neighbors

Glass shatters against the wall.

Kavya starts awake. She immediately looks at the man sleeping soundly next to her. A breath of relief. She looks around their small flat. The moonlight colors the home with a soft blue. The air conditioning whirs. Nothing out of the ordinary. She lies back down, pulling the covers up to her chin.

A wailing noise echoes on the other side of the wall. The wall that their headboard is pushed up against. Kavya pushes up on her elbows to get closer to the distress. Another glass shatters.

"Ishaan!" She puts a hand around his arm and shakes him. He groans in sleepy reluctance.

"Mmhm?"

"Ishaan, wake up!" Her worry and panic tremble beneath her whispering voice. He gets up and surveys Kavya's body, looking for anything of note.

"What is it?! Are you okay?!"

"I think something is happening with the neighbors." Ishaan immediately relaxes and throws his head back.

"God, Kavya! I thought something happened. Go to sleep."

He curls back into his usual position. Kavya doesn't move; her ear still pressed to the wall.

"Something is happening. I heard something break."

"Kavya!"

"What?"

"Go to sleep."

He's right. It's barely three in the morning. They both have work later. Her neighbors' affairs are none of her business. She lays back down. Ishaan immediately pulls her closer and tightens his grip on her, laying his chin in the crook of her shoulder.

"Good night, Kavya."
"Good night."

Kavya closes her eyes. There are no more sounds on the other side of the wall. Those neighbors have never been a problem. They are quiet and respectful. Kavya has only met the woman who lives there. The wife. Girlfriend? Whomever: she's very tall. And slim. Looks to be ethnically somewhere from the Balkan States. They happen to just come home at the same time as they both walked from the elevator to their respective flats, and she was carrying about six bags worth of groceries. Kavya contemplated asking if she needed any help, making note of the woman's slender arms and how her back hunched over as she attempted to hold everything while she unlocked her front door. Kavya didn't say anything. And that was that. The woman just gave her a small smile and entered her flat. Kavya wouldn't have even thought she was married or with someone but apparently Ishaan has bumped into him a couple times in the building's gym: "nice guy."

Kavya loves this building. It's modern and clean. The building has very few issues, and if there are, they get resolved quickly enough. The neighbors are kind, and most people keep to themselves. It's close enough to work for them both; 15 minutes for her, maybe 20-25 for him. It was the first place she moved into with her husband. She didn't know him well. Or this part of the city well. But this building held her hand during the transition. Allowed her the solace to fall in love with the man sleeping next to her. This is where she got to know her husband. His likes, his dislikes. She wouldn't have known tomatoes were not okay before their wedding. Or that he would wake up at the crack of dawn to watch cricket. Or that he refuses to watch any movie based on a book he loves. She looks forward every day to coming home from work and sitting down with him on the sofa, getting to know him more. It was comfortable. He was comfortable.

Yelling. Kavya moves towards the wall as much as her husband's grip allows her. She presses her ear as close as she can to the wall and listens.

Kavya has no issue with the different accents. After two years, she's been able to decipher the difference in dialect. The way Americans push their words together. She should be able to understand them. But under the guise of wails, it comes out as a garbled mess. What could possibly have her so upset? She's only able to hear the woman though. She yells at him through her sobs. Only when Kavya focuses enough, pushing away the sounds of the air conditioning and Ishaan's soft breaths, does she hear his low grumble. It's barely audible. She's not able to pull any words out of it. He might as well have been growling, a deep vibration resting at the bottom of his throat. The hairs on Kavya's arm stand. She shifts closer to Ishaan.

The woman is still crying. Through closed lids, Kavya pictures that overwhelmed woman she saw in the hallway.

More yelling. No. She's screaming.

"Ishaan!" Kavya is no longer whispering. "Ishaan!" Her husband gets up in a haste.

"What?!"
"She's screaming."

Ishaan leans toward the wall, mirroring his wife. He listens for a moment before saying, "I'm sure it's fine."

"She could be hurt, I heard glass break. Like something was thrown at the wall."

"Kavya, it's okay."

Another scream.

"Shut up! Shut the fuck up." His voice causes Kavya to shudder. A muffled scream, as if a large hand covers her mouth, follows the growl. She immediately gets up and looks for some clothes to put on.

"What are you doing?" Ishaan's eyes are barely open. He watches his wife run to their dresser.

"Kavya, what are you doing?" He is more stern, clear. Whatever sleep that lingers in his voice dissipates. "Kavya."

"What?!" She turns around, putting on a pair of pants. "We have to help her, Ishaan. She could be hurt."

"What?! Are you mad?! Stop." Kavya looks for her shirt. "Kavya, stop!" She freezes. "You're not going over there."

"Ishaan, please!"

"What if you get hurt?! Whatever is happening is between them. They will sort it out."

"Do you hear them? She's not upset. She's in pain."

"Then she'll call the police."

Kavya's eyes widen before she darts for her phone. Ishaan immediately snatches it from the charging port before she reaches her side of the bed.

"*We* are not calling the police. She will."

She looks at him incredulously. Doesn't he hear her cries, her screams? How can he—how can they not do anything?

"What are you talking about?"

"We are not getting involved, Kavya."

"What if he's hurting her?"

Ishaan swallows. "They will sort it out. Maybe this happened before. Or maybe it hasn't. Either way, they will figure it out."

Kavya doesn't move. Her disbelief immobilizes her, standing next to the bed. Ishaan looks at her pleadingly. "What if he kills her?"

"He's not—" He pinches the bridge of his nose. "Nothing will happen. They will be fine. She will be fine. We cannot interfere."

"Why?"

"What if it's nothing to worry about? What if it's just the TV?"

"It's not the TV, Ishaan!"

"Ok, ok. But what if this is just a couple's quarrel?"

"What if it's not? What if she needs our help?"

"It'll be fine!"

"You don't know that!"

More wailing. Straight from her diaphragm, it tears through the night as if she is right next to them. Kavya rummages for her shirt. She pulls it over her head, threading her arms through. As her eyes start to emerge from the hole, she sees Ishaan standing in front of her.

"Do not interfere, Kavya. I'm not going to tell you again. Please." Kavya stares at him.

"Please! PLEASE! I'm sorry!" The woman's voice is lower than Kavya expected. She imagined her with a lighter timbre, airy and bright. Spring initially came to mind for some reason, but these cries were nothing spring-like. *"PLEASE!"*

Kavya can only look at her husband. He hears her pleas. How can he not? She can see it in his eyes. His heart breaks for that woman. Kavya uses the distraction as an opportunity to move around him. She barely moves a couple of feet before his hand grips her wrist.

"Kavya."

"Please. Listen to her. I need to do something."

"They will sort it out."

"What if he hurts her?"

"What if he hurts you?!"

She knows he thinks she is fragile. Like the glasses shattering against that wall. But the stories she had heard. The quiet cries she would find throughout her family's building. It was always better not to interfere. To keep to themselves. And that was best. She saw the same neighbors the next day, flashing a smile at young Kavya, as if everything in the world was perfect. It made her feel like she was insane. Was she imagining it? Days went by before she heard it again. And she always did. And again, the next day, another smile. It became a pattern, one that was never spoken of.

She told her mother.

"Tsk, why are you thinking of other people's problems? Think of your own." And would move on with her day.

Kavya remembers a few days before their wedding. She was running late for dinner at his family's house. The calm before the storm. Ishaan lost it. He kept calling and calling. Everyone's phones in the car had lost signal. The traffic was relentless, barely moving an inch at a time. She only saw those calls as they exited into the city. Ishaan was so worried about his bride. Had she been in an accident? Was she having second thoughts? It consumed him for the three hours of radio silence. When Kavya and her family finally arrived, Ishaan relaxed but his mom remained tense. The food had gotten cold, everyone was tired and hungry. It was ten at night. His mom was always a caring woman. But that day, perhaps it was wedding fatigue and hunger, she had made some off-handed comment to Kavya's mom. She threw out another comment. And another. Soon, it escalated into a full-blown argument. Well, kind of. If back-to-back passive-aggressive comments count as an argument. Kavya thought about interfering, but Ishaan simply made eye contact with her and shook his head.

"No need to aggravate anything this close to the wedding."

Kavya agreed. Not to mention, she too was dealing with wedding fatigue and hunger. But the tension lingered throughout the festivities. In retrospect, Kavya wonders if it was better for them to argue. For them to blow up and leave the tension there. She's sure Ishaan hasn't thought about it since.

Kavya can only stare at her husband. The wailing sobs of the woman next door pour into their flat, drowning out the light buzzing of the air conditioner.

"Then you come."

"No."

"Ishaan."

"No, Kavya!"

"If you come, maybe nothing will happen. He'll stop. She can call the police."

"Kavya, I frankly don't care."

"What?!"

"I'm not risking you being anywhere near that man."

"We live next to them!"

"And you've never met him. I'd like to keep it that way."

She considers asking him if he'll go, but she doesn't want to. She doesn't want him to go. She cannot argue with him because she won't let him go either. She's never met this man. If he's taller than the woman, then he's for sure taller than Ishaan. She knows he goes to the gym regularly, so he'll have to be considerably fit. She definitely won't be able to hold her own. Not with her 5'1" frame. Will Ishaan be able to? She doesn't care to find out.

Maybe it is best not to interfere. To mind their own business. Let each household tend to itself.

"Can we at least call the police?'

"Kavya, what if we are just aggravating it by calling them?"

"What if we save her?"

Ishaan contemplates for a moment. He looks at his wife.

"Okay."

Kavya exhales at the word. Ishaan walks to the bed and takes his phone, unplugging it from the charger.

A large *THUD*. Kavya and Ishaan's heads whip around to the source of the sound. The same wall that their headboard presses against. Nothing. No wailing or screaming. No low growls. No glass shattering. Nothing. Nothing to fill the room but the whirring of their air conditioner.

Quiet

It's interesting, isn't it? How can one feel everything and nothing all at once? Overstimulated in absolute stillness. Just for a moment before the thoughts and emotions settle into place the way they are supposed to. Each one lining up accordingly as she processes through each one. All eventually leading up to what is acceptance.

Well, she's far from acceptance.

Gas station bathrooms are absolutely disgusting. She typically hovers. Now… she doesn't care. Her aching thighs gave out as soon as she saw the little piece of plastic. It dances on the very tips of her fingers. As if it's not real. But the two little blue lines are as real as can be. Stark and cleanly shaped, carved out by the white. It's supposed to just be one line. But there are two. One. Two. Sonia continues to stare. Perhaps, she is seeing double. But every time she refocuses, it's the same two lines.

Quiet. She wants quiet. Just for a second. But the cars whir past. The bell of the front door rings. The exhaust is blasting. Just for a second, she wants silence.

Her phone dings:

"sonia where are you"

Cars. Bells. Exhaust.

"getting gas…be home soon"

She clicks send before she even has time to call her mother and cry. To say she's sorry and doesn't know what to do.

Sonia remembers her English teacher in the 9th grade. How she kicked all the boys out of the room for the last five minutes of class. *Okay, ladies. I know you're growing up. And it's a tough time with all these changes. But you're also grown women.* Her classmates snickered. *But just remember, if you're in need of anything, you'll always have resources available. And you'll always have people by your side.* She had handed out a pamphlet, with a white woman and a nurse smiling on the front. That was only five years ago. And for the life of her, she could not remember if she even looked through the pamphlet. All she can recall is that white woman smiling with her perfect teeth. But she remembered throwing it out in the trash outside of the classroom the second the bell rang. Regardless, it wasn't like she needed it anyway.

Her father is sitting in the living room when she enters the foyer of her home. The television plays loudly. An array of papers lies scattered across the table. Reading glasses delicately balance on the end of his nose as he sorts through the mess. Sonia continues towards her room. He barely looks up as he calls her name.

"Sonia?"

She turns to him. Every muscle tenses to keep herself standing still.

"Where were you?"

"I was getting gas."

Her father continues to sort through the chaos before him. If he looks up, she wonders if he could see it in her. The change. The lack of self.

"For so long?"

"There was a long line."

He glances at his watch.

"Shouldn't have gone during office hours."

"Yeah, my mistake."

"Don't push it off next time."

Perhaps, it's for the best he never looks up.

It isn't until Sonia is in her room that she can finally exhale. She wants to believe that once she is back in this room, in her own personal sanctuary, she will feel better. But all the tears she holds in. The screams caught in her throat. The breath she keeps in. They hold on for dear life, and they won't let go.

Sonia has only cried a handful of times in her life. She's always been the pillar of calm. Her mother beamed when an older woman called her a "*dream baby*" on a flight to Frankfurt. She was often easily distracted. She would fall and her lip would wobble. Her mother would bring her a once- forgotten toy and present it as brand new. She would curl into her mother, and within 30 seconds, she'd be back to normal.

Today, she doesn't cry.

Silver anklets chime. Metal rings slap against the wood flooring. She anticipates the arrival as the chime and clinking metal grow closer. Not one to maintain the sanctity of personal space, Sonia's mother bursts into the room.

"Where were you?"

She sighs. "Getting gas."

"Oh, okay."

Sonia doesn't say anything.

"What happened?"

"What? Nothing…just tired."

"Did you eat?"

"I'll warm something up."

Her mother looks at her for a moment; whatever she intends to say is quickly brushed off with a simple "Clean the kitchen."

Her family isn't one for niceties, but the classic *cut the shit, here's what I think* type of people. She hadn't noticed how desensitized she had become to the bluntness until she went to college. She saw how everyone smiled, flashing their inexplicably white teeth, and not say anything negative.

"Oh wow, I love that dress!"
They most certainly did not love that dress.

Or, *"oh my god, I missed you."*
They didn't so much as think about you or even realize you were away.

It was something she had to get used to. She learned to smile with her not-as-white teeth and play through the niceties. And then…once they were in the privacy in their own dorm room, the white teeth would grow into fangs. Sonia feared what they might have said behind closed doors.

If there was one thing Indians and Americans had in common, it was the gossip—the exhilaration of hearing about other people's demises, never their successes. Only with her family and the ones in their community did they skip the "I love that dress" or the "I've missed you." No, they would simply look at you, their mouths curving into polite smiles that never seemed to reach their beady eyes. And suddenly, your insecurities and failures are thrust into the foreground of your painted portrait. Somehow, you find yourself returning the polite smile back. Next thing you know, someone complains about "how far these kids have strayed from the culture". When, in fact, that polite smile back is the most in tune with the culture you've ever been.

The steady rhythm of the knife Sonia rocks back and forth brings her back to reality.

Quietly chopping onions, her mother cooks next to her. "See, I don't see an issue. But she does…"

Her mother continues talking about a girl and her mother, but Sonia can't bring herself to listen. She feels her mother turning towards her to see if she is listening. A few "mmhm's" allow her mother to continue.

Women in their community never seemed to pass the mark or truly meet the requirements. Never seemed to truly meet the requirements. Men had their own expectations, but once met, they were admired. If they had a good job, went to a good school, and provided for a family. But with the women and the girls, it was like nothing could make them perfect. Even if they knew how to cook, were educated with a good job, got married, had kids at an appropriate age, were kind and hospitable, and maintained all the femininity they could manage—they would find something to bring them down.

Her parents aren't vicious or horrible. They were loving. They applauded everyone's achievements. But failures always find a way of invading conversations.

"It's so sad."

She can't recall the last time her mother worked in silence. It was either the constant chatter or music videos blaring on the TV—punctuated by the clanking of pots, the whistle of the pressure cooker, and the sizzle of oil.

"They've come all the way here for their children to prosper. And she ran away with some American?"

She was simply enjoying her independence for the very first time. She hadn't even kissed someone before going to college. But in the sea of Kirkland beer and hard liquor, deafened by a "lil'" someone booming through the speakers, she found herself enjoying the simple things. The bubbly laughter, ignited by nothing but the moment. The reason to dress up every week. The escape. The excuse to just be. Why shouldn't she have enjoyed it?

"And she was very hardworking. Do you remember? She was going to medical school. Who knows what that man does?" Her mother keeps an eye on her daughter as she carries on with her tasks.

She can't say he was very exciting as a man. He was handsome, albeit a tad slow. They had only been texting for some time, but soon after the first week of back-and-forth dryness, she figured this man wouldn't ask her out on a date.

He wouldn't have ever picked her up or bought her flowers. It wasn't until that liquor-infused night on the last week of the semester that they somehow clicked again. That night, he seemed to want to be in her presence. And maybe it was the liquor, the attention, or something less complex— something more animalistic —but she wanted to be in his presence, too.

"I guess it's her choice. She's going to be very disappointed in the end. But how can you do that to your mother? Just talk."

"Maybe her mother was being difficult," Sonia mutters. Her mother's eyes dart to hers. Sonia quickly averts.

A beat passes before her mother clicks her tongue, "Everyone is difficult; you cannot just run away."

Maybe it was a fluke.

She has seen on numerous occasions how false tests come up. Okay, she's not seen it. But she can hope, right? She remembers the name on that pamphlet from all those years ago. That honestly was the only name she heard. She opens the doors and is invited by an awful chartreuse smeared on the walls. There was no one else in the waiting room. Cars zoom by outside, tires screeching and horns honking. She recalls the smiling white woman on the cover. How safe and secure she must have felt…

A sneering woman sits behind a bulletproof glass at her desk. *Clack, clack, clack*—her acrylics dance on the keyboard. It isn't until Sonia steps directly in front of her that she looks up. She seems young, but gravity hasn't taken long to pull at her ski. She also seems to be a bitch.

"How may I help you?"

Sonia takes a breath. "I'm pregnant and need an abortion."

The woman seems unfazed by the words Sonia hasn't been able to bear uttering for two weeks. The woman staples some papers, clipping them onto a clipboard.

"Okay, fill this out, please. We'll have to confirm with a blood test before we proceed."

Sonia simply nods and takes the clipboard.

Does she have a history of heart disease?

Her mother would fill out all the questions for her while Sonia wat the muted *Finding Nemo* playing on the television hung in the lobby.

The gaps in the form made it clear why she had to do this. She hesitates before handing it back. The woman doesn't give her a second glance.

"Take a seat."

~

The blood test confirms it. Took them a couple of days. Somehow, she knew, even before the needle pierced her arm, before that filthy gas station bathroom, she knew. And she hoped to have been proven wrong. When her phone dings at dinner, the words "POSITIVE" push like one of her father's lectures. The type that says the same thing over and over again. Where you get to the point and say *I get it,* but it just keeps coming, like a punishment within itself.

~

She got out of the house three days later. Excuse of choice: she needed to go to the library to apply for internships. Her parents never deny that. She came back to the beaten clinic. The Bitch was still at the desk. She didn't recognize Sonia.

"Hi, I received my blood test results?"

She hands over her ID. The Bitch clips a piece of paper to a board and slides it toward her.

"Can I have your insurance card?"
"Actually, I was hoping to just pay for it?"

She looks her up and down. Sonia feels ice creeping through her veins under her gaze.

"Do you have insurance?"

"Yes, but –"

The Bitch shrugs and proceeds to clack her acrylics on her keyboard. She prints out another paper.

"Okay, it's $800. We take credit." Sonia gapes. "I'm sorry?"

"It's $800 if you're paying out of pocket." "So, will insurance pay for it?"

"It might."

Sonia ponders for a moment. She's in college. She certainly does not have $800. She's got exactly $353.46 in her savings and $12.58 in her checking. What would she tell her parents? What if they don't find out? What if they find out? In either scenario, she is getting scolded. At least in one, she's not bouncing a babbling, biracial baby on her hip.

She hands the woman her insurance card. She's never had to take it out before. The Bitch clacks her acrylics once more, then looks back at Sonia.

"You're out of network."

"What does that mean— "

"It means we don't take your insurance."

Sonia isn't one to panic. She is rational—the way her parents taught her to be. She approached things with caution.

Well, clearly not enough.

~

Sonia looks at herself in the mirror. Her room, decorated in the chaos of her youth, engulfs her small frame.

The walls are painted pink. Her collection of Harry Potter books sits untouched on a small bookshelf. Photos of her family and friends are scattered across the walls. A stain, splattered on the carpet, from when she opened a shaken Coke can. As a child, when her mother was pregnant with her younger sister, Sonia would stand in front of the same mirror. She would push her stomach out and stare at herself. She would delicately place a hand on the top, just like her mother.

Chime. Metal. Her mom enters her room.

"Hi."
"Hi, did you – what happened?"

Her mother studies her face.

"Nothing." Her mother's eyes narrow. "Did you put your clothes in the dryer?"

"No, I'll do it right now. Sorry."

A moment passes.

"What happened?"

"Nothing, Mom."

Her mother stares at her. Sonia doesn't look at her. Whatever expression was painted on her mother's face is unreadable.

"Go put your clothes in the dryer. They'll start smelling. Sonia, I'm not going to tell you again." Sonia's mother doesn't look back at her daughter as she leaves the room. Sonia doesn't move. Her mother comes back in.

"What are you doing?"

"Mom, I'm coming. I said I'll do it."

"But you're not doing it. You're still sitting."

"If you gave me a second, I would have gotten up."

"Sonia, you need to have more responsibility. This is such a simple thing."

"I said I'll do it!" Sonia's voice cracks.

"What do you even do in college? Do you just let it sit in there?"

"No!"

"Don't raise your voice at me."

"No, I don't," Sonia says softly, her chin trembling.

"You must be more responsible. I'm not always going to be there to remind you and take care of you. There are so many girls in your year that are working this summer. At least, have some responsibility at home." Her mother mutters to herself as she leaves the room.

The thought that anyone would know made her nauseous. She had friends. She had her family. All of whom she loved. She cared about them. And she knows that if someone came to her, she would help them. But the sheer thought of them looking at her, then down at her stomach, then back at her. How would they perceive her? Who would they tell? Nothing would be hidden. Someone would tell someone. And then she would be forever tainted. For once, she prefers the fake niceties of her college friends. She would be fine with pretending if only it were to alleviate the sinking feeling.

That feeling that she has done something wrong. Each muscle in her body contracts as if punishing her. The nausea. The fatigue. Punishment. The feeling of being locked in a room with no windows while everyone you love is on the other side of the wall having a party, all while her organs are turning themselves inside out. It's her punishment.

This isn't ever a conversation with anyone. No one ever spoke about what would happen if someone were to get pregnant. No one ever spoke about pregnancy before marriage. No one even spoke about sex. All Sonia knew was that it wasn't supposed to happen. It wasn't allowed. She doesn't even know what her punishment would be. Would she be kicked out of her home? Would she not be allowed to go back to college come August? Would everyone in her community know? How would they see her?

Someone shameful? Someone broken? Someone too ruined to be seen?

~

God bless the internet.

While her predicament may not be spoken about in their community, there are certainly others who do. Numerous women list out their experiences. Detailing the pain. The loss. The loneliness. The relief.

She pities the women highlighted in the stories. She praises them. She knows them. They weren't all teenagers. Some were moms. Working women. Black, White, Indian, East Asian. Some were married. Some were not. Some were young. Some were old. Some had gone through the more well-known methods of practice. Others had not.

Bright colors. There are no pictures. No smiling white women. But it's clear. This service is here for one reason. Plain and simple.

$250. That was all she needed. That was most of what she had. But she had it. She could stay in her home. Not make some excuse for making her way out again. She could lock herself in her room.

After everyone's asleep. Finish this. And then, this foreign feeling in her stomach will dissipate. And she will be okay.

Six. Seven. Eight. Eight weeks. By the time she followed all the steps, her package is in the mail at eight weeks. Sonia all but camped out by her mailbox, making sure she got the package before her parents did. It had been eight weeks. They would already have their little fingers and toes. Their nose, a bit sharper. The lips are starting to push out.

Sonia wonders how they would look. If they would have their father's eyes or their mother's ears. If they would have her thick dark hair or his light brown. If they would be a boy or girl.

A part of her wishes she knew the person growing inside of her.

She hides the tiny, unassuming package in her jacket as she walked back home.

"Why are you wearing a jacket?"

Sonia turns to her father, once again sorting through some paperwork on the kitchen table. A never- ending task, it seems.

"I was cold earlier."
"It's in the 80s today."
"Yeah, Dad."

Her mother is on the other side of the kitchen. A pressure cooker sits on the gas as she cuts up an assortment of vegetables.

"Sonu," her mother calls to her, "what are your plans for today?"

"Um, I don't have any plans."

"Nothing?"

A loud hissing whistle bursts from the cooker, startling Sonia. One.

"No."

"You should go see if Maya is free or something."

"Why?"

"She's home too, no? You won't be able to hang out with her when you're both away."

"Yeah, maybe later, I guess."

Sonia looks at her father, who is already lost in the sea of papers before him.

"Did something happen?" Her mother asks.

Another *HISS*. Sonia jumps. Two.

"What do you mean?"

"I'm asking if something happened. You can tell me." She genuinely wishes she could.

"No."

"You seem down for the last couple of weeks."

Sonia looks up at her mother for the first time in weeks. She examines the creases near her eyes, her lips that have gradually thinned over the years, and the few grey hairs she somehow missed the last time she colored her hair. Sonia was always told she looked like her mother. The photos of her mother as a child and photos of Sonia at the same age— the only differing factors are the decay of the older photos.

She's what she will look like when Sonia is a mother and a wife.

"Everything's fine. I'm just tired and cold." Her mom walks over to her and presses a palm to her forehead and neck. Sonia stiffens under her touch, frozen in place.

"You need to eat better, beta," her mom looks into her eyes. As if she's trying to decipher her. To break her down.

"Yeah, got it… I'll be upstairs."

Sonia didn't wait for whatever comment her parents would've made. About spending all her time in her room. About dismissing them. Any other day, she would feel the guilt building up. The lying, the rudeness, the disrespect. She pushed it off as pregnancy hormones. She can make it up to them when she's okay.

Eight weeks. Size of a lemon, she read. Sonia hastily opens the small package. Two pill bottles drop out. She takes out the instructions and reads it. She reads again and again until she's able to memorize every word. One pill she was supposed to take immediately. She takes it, gagging along the way. She remembers how her mom would help her with the antibiotics she took as a kid. Her mother made sure to carry large water bottles everywhere they went. She remembers how she, as nine years old, would chug water in the backseat of her mother's SUV just to get that medicinal powder to be swept off her tongue. She didn't have a large water bottle. Just the cup next to the sink. 8 ounces was nowhere near enough.

24 hours. She had only 24 more hours. Then, the second bottle. The four pills she would need to take.

Dinner is calm. Her parents try to start a conversation, but it dies as abruptly as it starts. All Sonia could think about was those two bottles sitting upstairs. She felt that tight sensation in her lower abdomen. The feeling she assumed she must have gotten used to over the past couple of years, but still, it continues to surprise her. The sensation only seems to get tighter and tighter, pulling her organs in towards one another.

The next day, Sonia stays in bed. She doesn't come down until the early afternoon. She's sure her parents must've said something. Something about being lazy and not making use of the day. But her brain is too consumed with the volume of the house. No wonder her parents' voices are naturally several decibels higher than most people's. The refrigerator whir loudly. The sportscasters on the television scream. Doors bang. The clanking of cookware. The air conditioning is blasting. The creaking of the doors. It was too much. Just for a moment, she needs silence.

That night, Sonia looks through the instructions again. No matter how many times she's read it. She will read it again. Just to make sure. She reads the side effects—bleeding, cramping, nausea. Perhaps a man would be concerned. She is old enough to know the normal symptoms she goes through every month. She double-checks for the sanitary products she keeps in her bathroom. She makes sure to put a towel down on her bed. She's ready. For eight weeks, she's been ready.

Midnight. While everyone else has fallen asleep, the house remains awake. The whirring, the blasting, the creaking. Sonia lays in her bed, pulls off her pants and underwear, and grabs the second pill bottle hidden under her pillow. Four pills. Just four more. Sonia takes one at the tip of her finger and carefully makes her way down her body. Her finger hesitates for a moment before she pushes it in, dry and cold. Sonia winces from the discomfort. She repeats for the second. And the third. And the fourth. Pulling her underwear and pants up, Sonia lays down and waits.

Nausea rises. Fast, gushing up towards her throat. She runs to the bathroom and throws up into the toilet. The tightening never subsides. It only gets worse, as if her body is trying so hard to fight it. Sonia rests her head next to the wall. Her gaze wanders down and sees blood dripping—cascading—down her leg and onto the tile. Her pajama pants cling to her thigh, stained dark. The thought of grabbing another sanitary napkin vanishes as her dinner once again rises to her throat. The tightening pain causes Sonia to keel over at the waist. The contracting pain of her insides. It's suddenly burning hot. Sweat starts to bead on her forehead. Somehow, she drags herself from the toilet to the bathtub, tugging a trashcan with her. With her clothes removed, she sits in her tub. The water runs, pulling the dripping blood into the drain. Her top half hangs over the side as her dinner continues to rise and is released into a bin.

Sonia has only cried a handful of times in her life.

Today, Sonia cries as she feels her body fight her. She cries as the pain suffocates her lower abdomen. She cries as she feels the loss of her body's creation. She cries and cries and cries.

~

She didn't know how long it had been. How long did it take for her to hear the faint chime and metal approach her room again? How long did it take for her to see the shadow loom over her bloody bathroom tile?

How long it took before a warm hand settled on her bare back, moving in slow circles.

And suddenly, the bathroom went quiet. Quiet. Quiet. Quiet.

Mother of the Bride

The second a nurse handed Radha her baby, all paths converged into one. In her youth, she could've been described as directionless: catching the nine to twelve with her friends, flirting with her classmates, driving her two-wheeler to God knows where just to get out of town for a little bit. In her studies, Radha did well, but everything felt like a chore. Directionless. But to be fair, it wasn't like she needed one anyway. Her daughter arrived with her large eyes darting around as if there was so much to take in. And suddenly, her life found direction. And it was thrilling. To have that awareness of what her life would become. When that newborn in her arms learns to walk, smiles on her first day of school, when she goes to college.

And today, that little newborn with the same large eyes is married.

After a year of planning and flying back and forth from India and the U.S., Radha didn't even register that her daughter wasn't coming home—that she wouldn't see her in her room after tonight. The same room she knows her daughter had been desperate to escape. The constant yelling and crying. The "I hate yous" and the "you're insufferables". Her son had never been like her daughter. He's always been the calm and quiet one, always assessing before reacting—like their father. He was committed to a career in aerospace, had made the dean's list, and was set to graduate magna cum laude. He was also tall.

But her daughter…she's different. Not one to assess but one to react. Loud in her thoughts. Something made even clearer under the weight of wedding preparations this past year. And she's only just realizing that after tonight, she'll sleep with the weight finally lifted.

And yet, she hasn't stopped crying.

Her daughter is dancing with her new husband in the middle of the dance floor. Her silver dress shimmers with every step and twirl. Light reflects off the sequins. The mirrored pieces of a disco ball cascade like liquid. In her childhood, Radha's daughter would absolutely hate wearing her traditional dresses. She would cry about the fabric scratching under her arms. She hated the weight. She felt clownish in the bright colors. And yet today, she's walking on air. Her skin is glowing. Her smile beams as she looks up at the man whose name she has taken. He smiles back at her. And Radha's daughter couldn't be any happier.

Her daughter's wedding is so drastically different from what Radha's had been. So much louder and grand. Of course, Radha's husband would've stopped at nothing for his little girl. Radha's wedding had 300 fewer guests than her daughter's. With only immediate family in attendance, the week blurred by in a rush to secure Radha's visa. Her husband had only so much time off, and he needed to get back to the States, preferably with his new wife in hand. They bought the first saree they saw.

She couldn't have cared less at the time and opted for an orange silk. Not even remotely close to the price point of her daughter's pedicure. The decor was simple, with a few plastic marigold garlands draped around her family home. They planned and executed an entire wedding within one week. Twenty-one days later, her husband handed her a one-way ticket—out of her home into her new life.

Her daughter, on the other hand, took her time planning her special day. She came to her parents with a detailed presentation, including a color palette (light colors along the lines of something called *"French Rocco Coco?"*;

budget breakdowns (home celebrations for the "boring" religious obligations to save money, budget allocations for a specific DJ); themes for each festivity (the sangeet theme of *Las Vegas* was floated around); and even floral expectations (absolutely no roses allowed on the premises whatsoever). It was the most effort her daughter had ever put into anything.

Her daughter and son-in-law finish their dance with a flourish. The crowd erupts into a startling applause. She wipes her tears and claps along with them. The DJ seizes the moment with a *boom* that echoes through the hall. Everyone cheers. The newlyweds begin pulling their friends onto the dance floor. Everyone gets up and starts to dance. Radha turns around and pretends to be busy with a flower arrangement. Alone in the corner, the commotion allows her to hide in plain sight.

The night her daughter confessed to five years of secrecy began like any other. They met towards the end of college and have been together ever since. They would sneak off on trips and have sleepovers, and they wanted to get married. Radha had never been angrier. So angry, she became lightheaded and dizzy. And she couldn't even say why. Her daughter automatically became defensive. She was so young. So naive. She didn't understand the efforts that followed that kind of commitment. After all, her daughter is directionless, just like she was.

She and her daughter had always been alike. They even had the same sharp nose that they both seemed to hate. As she was growing up, her daughter even resented the same foods as Radha. Foods that Radha had to pretend to like just so that her daughter could finish her meal. It wasn't until her daughter grew older that they started becoming different people. When she would never know if her daughter was home or not. When she would just drive off without telling anyone where she was going. When she coasted for most of her life. How could she coast when everything she wanted, she was given? She was able to do whatever she pleased. And yet, she continuously found fault in her as a mother.

She met him at a restaurant. Only a few weeks had passed since that night—since the night they screamed incessantly at one another since her daughter looked…different. Italian was the classy choice. And with an American man now apparently a part of the family, Italian was also a safe choice. When they shifted to their table, he held a chair out for her. It was a bit extravagant, to be honest, but her daughter just smiled as the rest of them eased into their respective seats. The conversation was light, flowing effortlessly as the dishes arrived. Radha and her husband asked him about himself—his work and background. Both his parents were doctors, supposedly. He asked them questions about their lives before the States, their interests and pet peeves, and stories about their daughter when she was a child. He was charming. He was tall and, sure, handsome. He seemed protective over her with their chairs so close to one another. It was that dinner where she decided she didn't mind him. The night of yelling and tears, just weeks ago, now forgotten. Radha supposed her daughter would do whatever she pleased, regardless of her approval.

Everything that followed hit Radha like whiplash. She saw the professional pictures capturing the moment he sunk his knee into the sand in front of her daughter, a diamond glistening from the afternoon sun while waves softly crashed into the land behind them. The shopping, the planning, the chaos that followed. And, to his credit, he was by her daughter through it all, despite not understanding a word of their customs and practices.

It had only been a few years since her daughter left for college, yet somehow, the time felt stretched and frayed between them. When she moved back home to save on rent, Radha expected some closeness to return—some semblance of familiarity. Instead, the distance masqueraded as presence. Piles of trash bags sat untouched by her daughter's door, plates hardened with dried-up food lay forgotten in the sink. There were days when Radha couldn't even tell if her daughter was home.

Despite eighteen years of raising her under this same roof, it was as if they barely knew each other.

There was a time when they did. When uneasiness consumed them, and they naturally gravitated to one another. When Radha would stand awkwardly while her husband entertained his co-workers.

She never knows what to say to Americans. She would make it through polite greetings, only to fade into the background. They would never know how lively she was or how funny. They would never know how much of a person she was. Not her husband's co-workers. Their neighbors. Or the other parents at the kids' school.

But her daughter would see her. She would drop whatever toys she would have been playing with and run to her. She would hold her hand and naturally ask the most arbitrary questions. Questions no child needed to have answered. But Radha would answer. They would sit in the corner of whatever room, and she would answer all her daughter's questions. The time would go by in a flash. No one would question the doting mother. No one would bother her and ask about the movies she didn't see or the politics she didn't understand. Before they knew it, her daughter would drift to sleep against her, and then it was time to go home. They would sit quietly in the car and her husband wouldn't have even known. Wouldn't have even registered how out of her element Radha was. How her lack of direction left her floundering at times, and how the simplest questions from her little girl brought her back.

Her daughter stands, mic in hand. Her husband holds her other hand delicately as he looks up at her. The dancing of the guests slows as the newlyweds smile at each other. "Thank you all for coming. It's a blessing to have you all here to join us on this day." Radha looks to her audience, listening intently. They seem enamored by her. Her gratitude. Her modesty. Her all-consuming love for her new husband. They laugh when prompted. Soft sniffling fills the pauses in between. Her daughter stands speaking out, so utterly confident and tall. Even if she weren't the bride, every gaze would be drawn to her. "I love you very much," she tells him in conclusion. "We never grew up together, but we get to grow together. And I look forward to being the people we are meant to be together." The couple share a kiss, wrapped in certainty and promise. The audience cheers, the pulsing of the room continues, and Radha's heart can't help but swell to the point of agony.

And Radha's gaze lingers on her daughter, watching as she wraps her arms around her husband. He whispers something in her ear, which prompts a large laugh as the two resume dancing. A secret only the two of them will know. Even with the vibrations of the room, it's just the two of them. She registers the way he looks at her daughter. Like he doesn't see the little girl she raised. He sees someone else. The person he gets to grow with. The person Radha no longer recognized.

And just like that, Radha is once again directionless.

Relevant Experience*

*(supposedly)

Ira has always been beautiful. The kind of beauty that was simultaneously admired and envied. Long, black hair. Big doe eyes. A large smile that spreads from ear to ear. Her beauty is her parent's pride and joy. Even now, as an adult, she walks down the street and feels the lingering eyes on her at any given time.

And it is invigorating.

Ira has no shame in taking advantage. The immediate acceptance, the free dinners, the kindness. She absorbs as much as she could in a short span of time. It was all she could do with what she knows.

There was never a question of who she would be in adulthood. But rather how lucky a man would be to have her. How captivating her children will be. It didn't matter how smart she was or how kind.

Ira's beauty. The first and only defining feature.

So, while her peers worked for their successes, her father bought an apartment for her on the West Coast. "For the experience," he said. She was agreeable as long as she got out.

Then came her new roommate, Rajvi. Her father supposedly connected with her on Facebook and set it up without Ira even knowing.

"Wasn't sure if you knew how to go about the process, so I just went ahead and found one for you," he said, absentmindedly on the phone when Ira called, alarmed to find a stranger in her new apartment.

"You should have told me," she muttered.

"Oh, please. We both know you wouldn't have handled it efficiently, and this was time-sensitive."

"Why was it time-sensitive?"

"Mortgage, interest–you wouldn't understand."

She probably wouldn't have.

Rajvi, on the other hand, is incredibly studious, and it paid off with her big, cushy job that had her moving into Ira's apartment. She is the definition of ambition. Waking up at the crack of dawn to work out when Ira was inexplicably tired at any given notice. Cooking healthy meals while Ira sticks to takeout. And while Ira was drinking and dating, Rajvi was building 401K.

Rajvi seems so innocent in comparison, and as sweet as she is, her presence only reminds Ira of the person she was built to be.

Oddly enough, Rajvi admires her for it. She has never seen Ira for who she was—the girl who never amounted to anything, the person who always seems to be ten steps behind, the woman who had her own father buy her an apartment, no questions asked, because even he knows she is a lost cause. Somehow, Rajvi just sees someone in love with life.

She decides to take her friend out on the town. Rajvi asks to borrow an outfit, deeming her own closet to be dull and lifeless. With Ira's clothes on, Rajvi seemingly inflates. She glows brighter. She doesn't walk; she glides. There was a sort of power in the two of them as they strut down the street.

"Damn girl!" Some loser calls out.

"Thank you! Have a nice day!" Rajvi chirps back, never breaking her stride.

As much as her father provides for her, the one thing she truly allows herself to be grateful for is Rajvi's presence in her life.

And while Rajvi embraces new experiences—men, friends, independence—Ira, in her own way, is learning to grow beyond herself and her past.

~

They grew up together. Only ten months apart. Somewhere, buried beneath the dust and long-forgotten toys, there exists a photo—him holding her as a newborn, his tiny arms barely strong enough to cradle her. She spent the duration of their three years together looking for that photo—knowing it would be her favorite, but to no avail. Even then, their moms would joke that one day, those two babies would marry. That they would all live together in one home with their grandbabies.

But somehow, they found their way to each other— all on their own.

"It wasn't until that semester in college when they spent every waking moment together. He was her first everything—first friend, first love, first partner. He was the only thing she ever knew. And he was the one she would have married, with that baby photo front and center on their save-the-dates.

But in their three loving years together, he badgered and questioned if her gaze would wander. If he was the only thing she knew, then wouldn't she want to know more? If she didn't revel in the attention that people always seem to give her. She spent her energy defending herself, only to realize at the very end how it was his gaze that wandered, and his incessant questioning had only masked his own guilt. He talked down to her, ensuring she never felt confident enough to seek someone else. He let her shine—displayed the beautiful woman on his arm—but never let her stray far enough until she could stand on her own and cast a shadow over him. He dismissed her to build a new life for himself. He took care of her. He comforted her. He loved her.

And she always did what she was supposed to. She played the perfect girlfriend, expected to be the perfect wife. Submissive when asked. Sexual when seduced. Quiet when provoked.

She practically ran out of his apartment that day. She barely glanced back as she turned the corner, catching sight of a matted, curly head watching her from the doorway. It wasn't until she stumbled into the elevator that she was hit with a tide of relief. There was no more senseless interrogating, no more defending, no more constant fighting. A tide washed over—pure, unfiltered befuddlement—as she wondered why she was so desperate to keep that insecure, 5'10" man in her life.

Somehow, that relief was short-lived. At one point, she dreamed of being a bride, a mother. Now, there was nothing left. No career goals. No partner. Nothing. And she got to an age where as much as she liked to drink and spend her night out dancing in the starlight, her friends outgrew it.

So, it was just Ira—with nothing and no one as the people she loved went on about their lives. And left her behind.

And as much as she was loved, she was never needed.

"So, what should I do?" Rajvi startles her out of her trance.

"Make eye contact with him, small smile, and then look away. You want to be interested but not enough," she tells Rajvi.

Rajvi looks back at the sea of young men with a glint in her eye. Ira proposed going out for Rajvi to meet someone naturally. As opposed to hiding behind phones as many their age tend to. Ira bumps her shoulder, egging her friend on. But she just keeps drinking her disgusting drink, supposedly the only drink Rajvi could stomach. Then, one of the boys makes eye contact with Rajvi. Ira rarely gets butterflies from men these days, but she'd be lying if she said she doesn't get butterflies when that man approaches her friend.

A stark contrast to the man who approaches her the moment her friend's attention drifted elsewhere. It became a game. What poor soul she would pretend to be interested in. And sometimes, she, herself, was the poor soul, though she would never have admitted that out loud. Her friends would laugh at her stories, at the men she would swipe on, at the suffocating dates she went on, and all the characters she would meet.

While her friends were all on track to getting happily married, Ira took the time to be her friends' entertainment…all while she felt ever so lonely and hopeless. It was exciting to them and, more or less, tedious for her. Ira would never say it out loud. But the game came with intention. It came with desire. And all she wanted was to feel loved. It was very soon after running out of that apartment that Ira realized that even when she was loved, she was never loved like them. Her friends, the people in her books, the couples she'd catch a glimpse of just walking by.

But then comes a man like this one. Argumentative, brash, so entirely in their own world that they cannot comprehend that the woman across from them is their own person, a whole being. Even if Ira, herself, was barely one.

Nah, I'm definitely funnier than you," he states boldly.

"I'm sure."

"Trust me, I could have you falling off your seat."

She wanted to respond with, *then, do it.* But, quite frankly, she didn't have the energy. Evidently, she didn't even need to respond because the Class Clown kept going.

She keeps an eye on her friend as he babbles. The slight brush of the arms. She smiles as he leans closer. As happy as she is for her friend, Ira envies Rajvi a bit. She misses the excitement of meeting someone new and the potential start of something new. Never mind the man next to her who just seems to be talking to her simply because he *can*.

What if she looks different? There's absolutely nothing of her personality that's remotely magnetic. She isn't intelligent or cunning. She isn't witty or charismatic. The only other defining factor is her being nice. But that is what is expected of her. What else should she be doing? What if people realize that her kindness is not for their benefit but her own—for how people perceive her? Even Ira, herself, wonders if she does the things she does purely for people to see value in her.

Eventually, at some point, you realize that time is already moving. People buy homes and move away; people fall in love and have children. Build their own stories.

And beauty withers.

Carved ridges along the skin. Black growing into white. Joints tightening.

It will all go away.

And Ira will be left with nothing.

"Damn, you could at least pretend to be interested," the Class Clown snarls. Impressive, he caught on so quickly.

"Sorry," she pushes out, "I'm just here to keep an eye on my friend."

She glances towards the bar, watching Rajvi. The boy returns her phone before pulling her into an embrace—Rajvi stiffens slightly before giving in.

Rajvi is ever-growing.

Her friend makes eye contact with her across the bar.

"My friend wants to leave. Have a good night," she excuses herself from the table.

The two friends make their way towards the door.

As the two sit in their rideshare, Rajvi beams at her phone. She turns the screen to Ira to show a message from a John.

"It was nice meeting you!"
"Text me when you get home okay :)"

Ira smiles. Her friend met someone sweet, it seems. Rajvi glows brighter as she is quick to text him back. All Ira can hope is that glow never dulls.

As her friend taps away at her phone, Ira embraces the silence and looks out the window of the back seat.

Buildings and signs blur past as Ira catches her own reflection looking back at her.

It's a faint reflection. She can barely see herself amongst the lights. But she can see the outline of her hair, her blurred skin, her lips, softly pouted, as she rests her face on her elbow.

There she is. Ira stares back. A dim echo. A beauty so revered; softly blurred and fading into the passing lights.

The Perfect Daughter

Tara hadn't expected the living room to look similar to the one she had already known. The living room where she spent the first 18 years of her life. The same room with the stained Persian rug, marked by a soda shaken open too soon. The same room with the old-fashioned stained glass window accents. The same room that was adorned in marigolds before her wedding. There were so many memories in this room. So many moments frozen in time with the little things left behind over the years. The magazines under the coffee table she used to read as a child to find her inner confidence. The old cable TV remote that fell behind the TV—never to be touched again. The peeling leather from the numerous times she was told not to put something hot directly on it.

Forty-five years of moments frozen in time. All in this one room.

And now, it's the room where her mother wandered in the middle of the night—and died.

They picked her up a few hours ago. Nobody knew what to do with her. But they took her. Now, it feels as if her mother's presence is burned into that Persian rug.

Her father found her. Just lying there. A glass of water shattered at her feet. He had woken early in the morning and sauntered downstairs, seemingly not even realizing she wasn't next to him when he woke up. He didn't feel the bed move. Didn't hear her footsteps. Didn't hear the shatter of the glass. No, he had a full night's rest. Within seconds, he managed to call everyone he knew: his children, friends, neighbors. By the time the police and EMTs arrived, the house was suffocating—crowded with faces, voices, and shock.

Tara barely got to see her when she and her husband arrived. They got the call earlier. She doesn't remember much of it. She doesn't even remember who spoke on the phone. Was it her father? Her brother? Or was it someone random? She doesn't remember her right knee splitting open when she hit the wood floor. The wound, struggling to heal, tearing open with every movement. She doesn't remember her husband hauling her up and into their car. The girls were at a sleepover next door. Thankfully, she wouldn't have to worry about that for at least a few more hours. She and Adhi arrived just as they were picking her up and taking her away. She didn't get to see her face. It was covered by the time she got there. Tara doesn't know if she even wants to.

"Papa?" Her father hasn't said much since she arrived. "Papa, do you want some tea?" He drags a hand down his face and nods. She counts the warm bodies in the room—twenty cups should be enough. She starts her process.

She wasn't sure why they were here, drifting through the house like ghosts. She grated ginger into the large pot. How long will they stay? How long will she and her husband stay? Who's going to take care of her dad?

"I'm gonna go pick up the girls." Adhi grabs his keys from the counter.

"Okay."

"What do you want me to tell them?"

"What do you mean? Just tell them what happened." There might be too much ginger in the tea.

"Yeah, of course. But what exactly do I say?"

"I don't know, Adhi."

"I think... we need to handle this carefully."

She leaves the pot to boil. Her energy comes in waves. One moment, she's determined, and the next, even simply standing feels too much.

"Just say what makes sense to you."

"Tara…"

"I don't know! Just do what you want!" She snaps.

Adhi doesn't respond. His eyes are glassy – after all, he loved her mother just as much. Adhi stares for a beat too long. What does he see? Who does he see? She's definitely not the same Tara as she was yesterday. He ultimately decides that silence would be the better choice before leaving. If only it wasn't.

Their long-time neighbor rolled up the carpet and put it in the garage. God, the floor was dusty and vacant. Despite the number of people in the house and the absence of the rug, nobody stepped into the area—as if the corners of that rug created an invisible, impenetrable wall. The rim of dust remained undisturbed, every single person walking around it. A part of her wished they walked through it just for the sake of normalcy.

The tea finally came to a boil. After pouring the milk and masalas, Tara started to sieve them in the multitude of mugs their family had collected over the years. The eleventh mug was one with a picture of her parents. One of those cringey 80s photo merchandise that was gifted to them when they first got married. Her mother was so young and so, so beautiful. Her father collected mugs—a habit, a ritual. A mug always came home wrapped and ready from every trip. Her mother would always get annoyed, claiming there would never be any space left. But despite it all, she managed to find space for every one of his mugs over the years.

Every part of her body is constricting. Each strip of muscle tightens, pulling taut, her bones vibrating beneath the strain.

The tea has too much ginger. She's not used to making it in such a large quantity. Tara consciously looks around to see the others drinking it. One aunty takes a single sip and sets the cup down—never picks it up again. Shoba Aunty sits next to her, putting a slim arm around Tara. She's Mamma's best friend.

They met once upon a time when they both emigrated to the United States. Their apartments were across the hall. Tara's mom was so excited about another Indian couple living so close by.

"Tara, sweety, the tea is lovely." No, it wasn't, but at least she gets a freebie today. How does she even answer that? Thankfully, she doesn't need to.

"Where are the girls?"

"Adhi is getting them. They were at a sleepover." Shoba Aunty clicks her tongue. "Poor things. Losing your Nani is always hard."

Tara just nods. "Adhi is telling them."

"Where is Shankar staying? With you, or will he fly back with Jay?"

She honestly didn't think of her father's living situation. He had always just been here. Him and Mamma. If anything, it was her and Jay making their way back every few months for whatever reason. She hasn't even spoken to her brother since three nights ago. She assumed someone had, and he was flying back to their hometown. She never even asked.

"Jay?"

"Your father called him. He should be landing soon, I believe." Tara nods.

"But I think your father should stay with you. With Jay's work schedule, he will need a little more attention, I feel. After all, you have your mother's touch." Tara knows it's meant as a compliment. Shoba Aunty has always been a lovely person. But the comment burns some part deep in Tara's chest that it could only be meant to inflict pain.

"Yeah, I'll talk to Jay and Papa about it." She doesn't know if she will.

"If you ever need anything, Tara, I'm here." She squeezes her shoulder one more time before sauntering over to her father.

She's never seen her father look so... old. He's always been fit—up at five in the morning for a run, never eating anything he isn't supposed to. Her mother, however, is different. She's a free spirit. She doesn't just enjoy; she indulges. She savors. Whatever meal is in front of her.

Wherever they go, she takes photos of the most random moments.

Tara wants her phone. Her mother's phone is full of indulgences her mother would allow.

Tara stands up from the couch. Her legs, surprisingly, feeling detached from her body. The front door opens again as she makes her way to the stairs. Adhi allows the girls to walk in front of them. They look so small. Only 10 and 8, Rani and Rhea now have fully formed personalities. They walk to Tara, and for the first time that day, Tara is grateful for the company. And all she wants is a hug. But the girls just stand there. Only after Adhi nudges them do the girls come forward and wrap their hands around their mother. Tara goes down to meet their level, split knee be damned. She squeezes their little bodies. And that tightening loosens ever so slightly. They smell of soap and linen, and she squeezes them more to show appreciation for Adhi having them bathe before coming.

She stands up, the girls still holding her hand. "You had them take a bath?"

"Oh, they must've been running around all evening with how they smelt."

"Thank you," she breathes out.

"Girls, go see your Nana. He'll feel better once he sees you." The older one takes the younger one's hand, and they make their way into the main room.

"How are you?" Again, with that damn question.

"Yeah, fine."

"I spoke with Jay in the car. He just landed."

"Do we need to go pick him up?"

Adhi shakes his head. "I already offered, but he had already ordered a car. Amy and the kids will come later, but he should be here soon."

Tara nods. "Okay, okay. I feel bad. I haven't spoken to him yet."

"He'll be here soon. It's okay." He rubs her back.

"The girls?"

"They seem to have understood. They kept asking 'why?' I don't know, it was a lot. Rani cried a bit, but Rhea seemed to absorb it all. Maybe it hasn't hit her yet. Or maybe she's just too young."

"Thanks for taking care of that."

"I also brought you a change of clothes and your toothbrush." Tara looks down. It hadn't even occurred to her—she was still in her pajamas, hadn't even brushed her teeth. She simply nodded once again.

"Um," she rubs her thumb against her eyebrow. "We need to figure out what to do with my dad."

"What do you mean?"

"He can't stay here, Adhi. And Jay lives in Chicago. Plus, he works all the time."

"So, he needs to come with us."

"I don't know. Shoba Aunty mentioned it. Obviously, I haven't spoken about it with Papa or Jay."

"What about Amy?"

"What about her?"

"I mean, the kids are a little older now."

"I feel like that's just opening up a whole thing. I don't know what the expectations are. With her or with him."

Adhi nods. "Yeah. Okay, okay. So... what about the funeral?"

"Oh God, I don't know Adhi."

"I just mean, have you spoken to your father."

"My father hasn't spoken to me since we came."

That tightness returns. Her body knots itself inward, pushing at her midsection like she could topple over at any second.

He hasn't spoken to her. Not once. Just vague nods, perfunctory responses to every other question. She hugged him, but he didn't hug her back.

No. He couldn't move.

She had just lost her mother, and he couldn't move. "What do you want me to do now?"

Tara looks at her husband. After 15 years together, they have figured each other out. But right now, she doesn't know anything.

"I don't know. Thank you for picking up the girls. And for the clothes."

Adhi nods solemnly. Tara glances over at her girls curled up against her father, his arms wrapped around them both. Rani has temporary tattoos all over her arm—

another detail she missed. Papa studies each one, tracing them with his finger.

"They're probably hungry."

"Shit. I meant to give them breakfast—I knew I forgot something."

"No, no, it's okay. I-I'll make something."

"Tara, I'll go pick up something."

"No—then it's weird if we only get food for them and not everyone else. It's fine. I can make like pulav or something."

"Tara, your mother just died. I think it'll be fine."

Leave it to her husband to put it so bluntly. Like there's no regard for their environment or the people loitering around. But it's true. Her mother is dead. She's not coming back tomorrow. Or coming downstairs. She just won't be here anymore. It doesn't matter what moments will be missed because they will never exist. Her mother, her mom, does not exist in this world anymore.

"I need her phone."

"What? Why?"

"I just— I just need it."

"Okay, it's probably upstairs, right?"

"Yeah."

"Should I get the girls something?"

"Yeah, fine. Maybe we can order pizza or something."

"Pizza?"

"I'm just trying to find something easy for all these people."

"It's just... pizza might not be the most appropriate. Considering the setting."

"It's food. It doesn't matter."

"Okay."

"Get whatever, Adhi. It doesn't matter."

A beat passes.

"You're okay?" She never will be. Not again. But what does it matter?

"Yeah, I'm gonna find her phone."

Tara makes her way up the stairs, leaving her guests behind.

Her mother's phone was left on the nightstand by her side as if she had just forgotten it and would come for it later. One of her father's mugs, with an old tea bag still in it, waiting to be washed. And her phone—unplugged from the charger, naturally. It would stress Tara out how often her mother's phone would die.

And, naturally, it's dead. The phone shakes in Tara's hand, and that constricting feeling comes back, threatening to incapacitate her.

"Tara!" Some Aunty calls from down. Tara lets out a shaky sigh. She reaches under the bed for the charger before plugging in the phone and heads back downstairs.

Jay has grown a beard. To be honest, she didn't even know he could do that. Her little brother looks stricken. The second they make eye contact, he pushes toward her. A sob releases itself from him as he folds his towering frame over her. She feels another hand on her back. In her peripheral, she sees another hand on her brother. Selfishly, she wants to shrug them off. To keep this moment—just for the one person who truly understands. But she doesn't move, and the hands stay. No tear escapes from Tara. And she doesn't let any words come out for them to be broken and lifeless.

She will hold her brother as long as he needs.

Time passes before he pulls away. She wishes he didn't. He moves towards the other people in the room. Tara makes eye contact with her father. Did he hug Jay? Did the shock dissipate enough that he hugged his son back after losing his mother?

The rest of the crowd moves back into the house with Jay. Only her father and Tara are left in the foyer.

"Papa, do you need anything?"

"No, beta. We should probably start on everything."

"Okay, yeah—"

"They got a death certificate when they came. And they have to do an autopsy because it happened at home. But you should reach out to the temple regarding funeral services."

"Yeah, once Jay settles in, we can give them a call."

"Look at him, Tara. He's too delicate right now. You've been so strong. After all, you're like your mother."

Tara doesn't say anything, but even then, she never seems like she needs to. Everyone seems to say it for her. Even after 43 years, she seems to just do and be whatever her loved ones need. Perhaps, she is like her mother.

Her mother didn't drive much in Tara's youth. She wasn't comfortable with these "crazy, American drivers." Slowly, over time, her mother had their father eventually teach her. It took her six months to learn how to drive. Her mother would humorously always say she would mistakenly turn on the wipers instead of the turn signal because she was so used to driving on the opposite side of the road. Six months, she took to learn how to drive. Her mother beamed the day she received her license, showing it to everyone she met. It was embarrassing for Tara. After all, most adults had their licenses. But her mother was so proud. And her mother seemed more fleshed out the day they got their new car. But she never went out on her own.

Tara remembers how frustrating it was for the first few years. How every speed limit was never exceeded, and every stop sign was treated like an actual stop sign. But she would take them wherever they would please. And she would wait however long they needed. And she would take them home whenever they were ready. No matter the time or distance.

She never knew why her mother suddenly decided to overcome her fear of American drivers or what that turning point was. In her youth, she would've thought it was purely to be able to get out of the house. Now, as a mother, Tara recognizes it had nothing to do with her mother's autonomy at all. After all, she, too, would take her girls wherever, wait for however long, and leave whenever.

She wants her mother's phone.

The girls run up to her at that moment. Pulling on the fabric of her pants.

She wants her mother's phone.

Her father is still standing in front of her. Both silently dissociating.

She needs her mother's phone.

Jay is here. What does he need? The girls continue calling for her.

She needs her mother's phone.

Where is Adhi? The girls keep tugging and tugging.

She needs her mother.

"WHAT?" Tara snaps at the two children, tiny hands tugging at her pants. She's so tired. She's so tired, and she misses her mother. She misses the only person who would help her.

Tighter. And tighter. Her body about to give out.

The girls whimper in response. Rhea's lip wobbles, her fingers tightening against her mother's pants.

"Adhi?" Her husband appears in the foyer. But the girls don't let go.

"What?" Tara asks more calmly.

"When are we going home?" Rani asks.

"Daddy will take you home."

"…I am?"

"Yeah, I don't know how long I'll be here for." She rubs a thumb against her temple.

She feels a tug on her arm as she is gently pulled aside—away from the children, her family, and the lingering eyes of her parents' friends. She sees Rani take her little sister's hand, leading her away from their mother. Adhi places her in a quiet corner of the house, his body blocking the guests. He grips her shoulders.

"What do you need?" Adhi searches her face. As if he could find something in the emptiness.

"I don't know."

"Do you want the girls to be here?"

"I don't know."

"Do you want to be here?"

She exhales, "I don't know," she admits.

A moment passes.

"Tara, you need to give me something to work with."

The rejection in his voice is palpable. And it breaks her heart. Her husband has always been the one who finds the solution. His engineering mind craves a solution. A way to break this down into something concise. Concrete. A thing that could be coded.

"I don't know."

Another moment.

"Can you take the girls home? They probably didn't sleep well last night." Adhi doesn't move.

"I'll see if I can get someone to watch them."

"No, no. It's fine. I'll come later."

"You're not staying?" She hears Jay's voice.

"No, I don't know." She turns to her brother.

"You should be with family at this time." An Auntie proclaims. Her own father's face looks at Tara the same way as her husband does. Searching, only to come up with nothing.

"We will figure it out," Adhi's voice is meant to comfort.

"I need her phone."

Adhi simply nods. "Okay."

She doesn't acknowledge her daughters as she pushes past them to go upstairs. She doesn't make eye contact with her father or her brother. And she doesn't look back at her husband as much as she wants to.

Her legs tire as she goes up the stairs. But her mother's phone lights up as she approaches it. She looks at the notification. It's just the news app.

Tara unplugs her mother's phone from the charger, then slowly sinks down the side of the bed until she's sitting on the floor.

The password has always been the same. It's always been Tara's birthday. Just like Tara's passwords have always been her eldest's. And Tara suddenly realizes—she doesn't even know why she wanted her mother's phone.

She opens the photos app. Photos of her grandkids. The meals she made. Scanned prints of Tara and Jay as children. Her friends. Her and her husband. Some are posed. Most are not. Some are blurry. Others have a thumb in the corner.

More notifications. Different messages. There were plans for next weekend. Someone called for dinner. A ticket to Chicago to see Jay's family next month.

More. A recipe for some custard she had intended to make was saved in the notes app.

Even more. It's like life didn't stop. That she would continue seeing her granddaughters every week. That she would go to that dinner next week. That she would see Jay in a month. She would make that custard.

She jumps from app to app—her mother's life still moving forward. Nobody knows. Nobody knows the Persian rug from the living room would get thrown away. Or that Jay would fly home. Or of her god-awful tea.

Nothing stopped. Her mother called yesterday. Tara didn't pick up—for some inexplicable reason. But it would've been okay.

Because she would've called again today.

And for the first time today, that tightening gives out. Muscles snap. Her skin loosens. And all the air packed into her lungs escapes in a choked sob. Tears well in her eyes, and her entire body shakes from the release.

And, God, it hurts.

She feels an arm close around her, and she falls into it. Tara's husband's scent envelopes her as she lets go. He doesn't say anything. Doesn't tell her that her daughters need her. Or her brother or father. He just holds her. And she's grateful.

She's grateful for once she is not someone's wife, or mother, sister or daughter. She is just someone who aches for her mother. For the woman who forged her. And the woman she no longer has by her side.

"My perfect daughter," her mother would say as she held a young Tara to her chest, once upon a time.

And the ache will never cease.

Acknowledgments

Thank you so much for getting to this point. Bear with me while I get a little sappy.

First, to my parents, Nisha and Sameer Surve—I joke that they only approve of my artistic endeavors because it's the only thing I'd ever be good at. But the truth is, their unwavering support is what keeps me afloat. Thank you for every word of encouragement, for being the pillar I needed, for shaping me into the storyteller I am today.

To my family, my extended Denver family, and my grandparents—Asha Jadhav, Sunanda Surve, Pratap Surve, and Satapa Jadhav—I'm sorry there are swear words in this book. But thank you. I've never had to face disapproval for being an artist or a writer—not in my family and not in my community. A rarity, I'm sure. But I am endlessly grateful for it, nonetheless.

To my book club sister, Georgia Johnson, who not only shares my love for romance novels but also generously combed through each word of this collection. Your insight refined these stories, your edits saved me from looking dumb with grammatical errors, and your friendship made the process that much brighter. I am indebted to you.

To a few of my friends—Hudah Rana, Raquel Rosen, Gayathri Gude, and Sharada Ramesh—thank you for reading along the way, for helping me shape these stories as I sat stewing in my one-bedroom apartment. This collection belongs to all of us. Your feedback, reassurance, and care mean everything.

To the Brand Library in Glendale, my quiet space—so many hours were spent here, surrounded by stories that came before mine. Also, thank you for your clean bathroom and water fountain. I'm sorry for all the wedding and quinceañera photos I've undoubtedly ended up in, being in the background of your picturesque building.

And finally, to everyone who picked up this collection and took the time to read it—thank you. Whether you're a dear friend, a family member, or someone completely new to my work, I cannot express how much your support means to me. I hope you got to see yourself in one of these characters.

Stories truly only live when they are shared. The fact that this exists beyond me means everything.

I hope you liked it. If you didn't, don't say anything.

About the Author

Krutika Surve is an Indian American writer, painter, and digital illustrator based in Los Angeles, CA. She grew up in Denver, CO, and is an alumna of the School of the Art Institute of Chicago.

Aside from her practice, she loves to read her romance novels, dance with her loved ones, and pretend to know a lot more about things than she actually does.

The Perfect Daughter is her first published work, but certainly not her last. Yes, that is a threat.

9 798218 717698